The Selected Works of Mahasweta Devi

Mahasweta Devi (b. 1926) is one of our foremost literary personalities, a prolific and best-selling author in Bengali of short fiction and novels; a deeply political social activist who has been working with and for tribals and marginalized communities like the landless labourers of eastern India for years; the editor of a quarterly, *Bortika*, in which the tribals and marginalized peoples themselves document grassroot level issues and trends; and a socio-political commentator whose articles have appeared regularly in the *Economic and Political Weekly*, *Frontier* and other journals.

Mahasweta Devi has made important contributions to literary and cultural studies in this country. Her empirical research into oral history as it lives in the cultures and memories of tribal communities was a first of its kind. Her powerful, haunting tales of exploitation and struggle have been seen as rich sites of feminist discourse by leading scholars. Her innovative use of language has expanded the conventional borders of Bengali literary expression. Standing as she does at the intersection of vital contemporary questions of politics, gender and class, she is a significant figure in the field of socially committed literature.

Recognizing this, we have conceived a publishing programme which encompasses a representational look at the complete Mahasweta: her novels, her short fiction, her children's stories, her plays, her activist prose writings. The series is an attempt to introduce her impressive body of work to a readership beyond Bengal; it is also an overdue recognition of the importance of her contribution to the literary and cultural history of our country.

The Selected Works of Mahasweta Devi

Mother of 1084
A novel. Translated and introduced by Samik Bandyopadhyay.

Breast Stories: Draupadi, Breast-Giver, Behind The Bodice
Translated with introductory essays by Gayatri Chakravorty Spivak.

Five Plays: Mother of 1084, Aajir, Urvashi and Johnny, Bayen, Water
Adapted from her fiction by the author.
Translated and introduced by Samik Bandyopadhyay.

Rudali: From Fiction to Performance
This volume consists of the story by Mahasweta Devi and the play by
Usha Ganguli. Translated and introduced by Anjum Katyal.

Dust on the Road: The Activist Writings of Mahasweta Devi
A collection of prose pieces.
Introduced and translated by Maitreya Ghatak.

Bitter Soil
Palamau stories by Mahasweta Devi.
Translated by Ipsita Chanda. Introduced by the author.

Our Non-Veg Cow and Other Stories
Translated by Paramita Banerjee. Introduced by Nabaneeta Dev Sen.

The Armenian Champa Tree
A novella. Translated by Nirmal Kanti Bhattacharjee.

Old Women
Two stories. Translated by Gayatri Chakravorty Spivak.

Titu Mir
Translated by Rimi B. Chatterjee.

The Queen of Jhansi
Translated by Mandira and Sagaree Sengupta.

Till Death Do Us Part
Five stories. Translated by Vikram Iyengar

Outcast
Four stories. Translated by Sarmistha Dutta Gupta

Chotti Munda and His Arrow
A novel. Translated and introduced by Gayatri Chakravorty Spivak.

The Book of the Hunter.
A novel. Translated by Sagaree and Mandira Sengupta.

BITTER SOIL

MAHASWETA DEVI

Translated by
IPSITA CHANDA

Seagull
BOOKS
CALCUTTA 2002

First printing 1998
Second printing 2002

Cover image: Chittrovanu Mazumdar
Design: Naveen Kishore

ISBN 81 7046 147 2

Published by Naveen Kishore
Seagull Books Private Limited
26 Circus Avenue, Calcutta 700 017, India

Printed in India by Laurens & Co
9 Crooked Lane, Calcutta 700 069

CONTENTS

'palamau is a mirror of india':
an introduction

mahasweta devi

THE STORIES AND NOVELS I wrote between 1976–1990 are very important to me. By then I had already published *Hazar Churashir Ma* (*Mother of 1084*), but had not written enough about caste and class oppression and exploitation. My reputation largely stands on certain works, of which the four stories in this collection, written in the 80s, form a major part.

I believe in documentation. After reading my work, the reader should face the truth of facts, and feel duly ashamed of the true face of India. To fully understand these stories, one must have a knowledge of agricultural economy and land-relations; because caste and class exploitation and the resistance of the exploited ones are rooted in India's land-system. I say 'India', though the location of these stories is Palamau. Palamau is a mirror of India.

For the benefit of the reader, let me explain the land-system I am critical of. In 1947 came independence. Systematic and thorough land reform by the Government, redistributing rural and urban land above the land ceiling to landless and marginal farmers, could have saved India from lop-sided development. This was not done. Only in two states, Kerala and West Bengal, was this system implemented and, to some extent, successful. The Government of India allowed the feudal land-system to remained unchanged in the rest of India. The upper-caste landowners are still as feudal as they were, abiding by values which are against women and the so-called lower castes. For the last five decades, one India has remained basically feudal, while the other has remained a victim of class and caste oppression. 'Land is not yours by right, land belongs to the privileged.' Belchi, Pipra, Arwal, Jehanabad—these names bespeak countless instances of land eviction of the poor, and brutal caste killings. In Andhra Pradesh, land belongs to different Raja or Zamindar agencies. That is why, since Telengana, there has been an ongoing violent people's resistance movement there.

Everything is for the upper classes. I, too, belong to that class. We had every opportunity to benefit from a good education, to be introduced to the world of art, literature and culture.

I saw with my own eyes the brutalities of the existing land-system. In one of my stories, 'Douloti', there is a character, Crooked Nageria. I saw this man, whose right side, from arm to ankle, was deformed. Why? Because he was a debt-bonded labourer. And, in the month of May, his *malik* made him lift a paddy-laden cart to take to the village market. He fell and his right side was crushed under the heavy cart. I asked the *malik*, Why not use bullocks? He answered, If a bullock dies in this heat, I lose a thousand rupees. He is just a bonded labourer. His life is of no value.

So the sole purpose of my writing is to expose the many faces of the exploiting agencies: The feudal-minded landowner, his henchmen, the so-called religious head of the administrative system, all of whom, as a combined force, are out for lower-caste blood.

That I have based my writings on truth, and not on fiction, is substantiated by the harijan killings and caste wars in Bihar, UP, MP, and other places. Read reports on Jehanabad and read 'Seeds'. 'Salt' goes even deeper, unearthing more of the root. The elephant and the tribal, both are expendable to the system. 'Shishu' (Little Ones) was born of tribal experience. My experience keeps me perpetually angry and makes me ruthlessly unforgiving towards the exploiters, or the exploiting system. That the mainstream remains totally oblivious of the tribal situation furthers that burning anger. And, in 1997, I find, in a page torn from *The Geography of Hunger* by the founder of the Nutrition Institute of Brazil, D. Castro, that my story bears out what he published in 1952. Chronic malnutrition has the result of stunting human and animal bodies. Pygmy horses found on Shetland Isle were exported to America for sale as dwarf-horses. But nutritious fodder helped these horses grow, and within three generations they were big and strong. The anthropologist Emil Tordey found tiny pygmies in equatorial Africa. Transferred to agriculturally rich areas, with a different climate, they slowly changed into normal-sized human beings. What I wrote in 'Little Ones' is correct. Starvation over generations can reduce ordinary-sized human beings to pygmies. Of course, the starving Aagariyas are savagely angry at a system under which some people eat three meals a day while they are forced to starve! For I believe in anger, in justified violence, and so peel the mask off the face of the India which is projected by the Government, to expose its naked brutality, savagery, and caste and class exploitation; and place this India, a hydra-headed monster, before a people's court, the people being the oppressed millions.

I have not written these stories to please my readers. If they get under the skin of these stories and feel as the writer feels, that will be reward enough. Incidentally, 'Seeds', 'Little Ones' and 'Salt' also feature my experiments with a language which is brutal, lethal at times. This was needed. These stories, written in the 80s, are becoming hideous contemporary realities every day in India. Whatever is written in these stories is continuing unabated. So where is the time for sleep? The situation demands immediate response and action.

little ones

THE NAME OF THE PLACE IS LOHRI, and it is situated at the *meeting point* of the boundaries of three districts, Ranchi, Sarguja and Palamau. *Officially* it's in Ranchi. But the entire area is a burnt-out desert. As if the earth here bears a fire of unbearable heat in her womb. So the trees are stunted, the breast of the river a dried-out cremation ground, the villages dim behind a film of dust. The earth is a strange colour. Even in the land of red earth, such a deep brownish-red is rarely seen. Of course, before fresh blood dries and congeals, it turns just such a dark, lifeless red.

The *relief officer* had been *briefed* before he came here. This *officer* is extremely honest and sympathetic. Rigorous elimination has gone into his final selection. He has been told that it's a damned terrible place. The inhabitants have no *honest way of living.*

—Why?

—They don't farm.

—Why? Do they have land?

The *relief officer* and the BDO were having this conversation inside the bungalow. Outside it is not yet cool. At night, the *chowkidar* will lay out string cots within the bungalow compound. Here no one sleeps indoors during the hot season. The *relief officer* has been appointed to do this work for just three months. He is on loan from the Food Department. Never in his life has he seen such an arid, uninhabitable place. The sight of those who come for relief, the near-naked, shrivelled, worm-ridden, swollen-bellied adivasi men and women, repels him. He had had the impression that adivasi men played the flute and adivasi women danced with flowers in their hair, singing, as they pranced from hillock to hillock.

Parking the jeep at the foot of a low hillock and climbing its gentle rise on foot, he has come to realize that it is not possible to run up hillocks. It makes one short of breath. He had the impression that singing played a big role in the lives of the adivasis. Now, he hears their songs for himself. Continuous, like the lonely wailing of an old witch. An extremely frustrating experience. The *relief officer* had formed a few ideas about adivasi life from films, especially Hindi films. If these are their songs, then how do they mourn their dead? These songs are like dirges. Unsettling! Unsettling!

—Why are they singing?

—They're *junglees*. Whatever happens, they think it's the work of evil spirits. They're singing to scare away the ghosts.

The very word 'ghost' is unsettling. The BDO

notices and smiles. Says—Did that scare you?

—No, no.

—This drought and famine are also the curse of the evil spirits, according to them.

—Oh.

—It's a godforsaken place. The Hindus live in decent spots, you'll find the flags of Mahabirji, the monkey god, fluttering in the air—none of that here. Oh, when will I be transferred!

—Where am I going tomorrow?

—Lohri is a terrible place. Even if you give those damned people land, they sell it off to the *mahajans*. They stare at you wide-eyed and ask, Where's the water? Where are the seeds? Plough? Bullocks? How can we farm? Even if you give them all this, they'll still sell to the *mahajan*, saying, What were we to eat until the harvest? So we borrowed money. Now, we've sold the land to repay the debt.

—Will I have to stay there?

—Yes. Set up camp there. You must stay. Get the camp going before you leave. I'll send men with you, don't worry, and on no account must you feel scared.

—Scared of what?

—Thieves.

—Thieves?

—Yes. Every time *relief* is sent, little boys and girls come and steal a sack or two of rice. Rice-milo-molasses, whatever they can lay their hands on.

—Little boys and girls?

—Yes. No one can catch them. A few people have seen them. Saw them myself, once. Had a gun with me, too.

—You carry a gun?

—*Licensed gun*. Lohri is a very nasty place. Ten years ago . . . no, it's twelve years now . . . there was a rebellion . . . fire . . . scorched everything.

—What're you saying?

The BDO says—I hadn't even got my job then. Do you know the story of this place, Lohri?

—No.

The *relief officer* knows nothing, and doesn't want to know. The demands of his job have forced him to leave the lights and glitter of Ranchi town to come here.

—Here, I mean in Lohri, lived the iron miners, the Aagariya. Legend has it that the Aagariya are of the demon *asur* clan. Their profession was to mine iron and forge iron implements. They ate flames, they bathed in rivers of fire, their settlement was Lohri. Their king's name was Logundih. The *asur* who lived under the earth allowed only the Aagariya to enter the netherworld and bring back iron. Only the Aagariya.

—Then?

—Their king was called Logundih. Logundih and his brothers were twelve in all. These twelve brothers had one wife.

—That's worse than Draupadi.

—King Logundih grew so proud that he thought he was more powerful than the sun god. The sun god came to Lohri. King Logundih, his eleven brothers, the settlement of Lohri, were all burnt in his flames. Their wife was in another village. She escaped. Smarting from the heat of the sun god's flames, she fled to a *gond's* house, and there, dipping into a pot full of curds, she cooled down. There under a *chhindi* tree, she birthed a son. His name was Jwalamukhi—he of the flaming mouth.

—*Baaprey!*

—When Jwalamukhi grew to manhood, he went to battle the sun god. They fought in Lohri, and the fever of their combat burnt the earth. During the battle, Jwalamukhi cursed the sun god—Only when the moon is full will you be able to mate with her. The sun god said—As for you Aagariya folk, all the wealth you earn from iron will turn to ashes. From that time, the Aagariya has been poor.

—A *junglee* tale.

—But of course. The Aagariya people are now in dire straits. Their hereditary caste trade, working with iron, is no longer theirs. But it is difficult to get them into farming. They say they are impure. Lohasur, the patron demon of iron, no longer gives them iron, nor does Koilasur, the demon of coal, allow them any coal. Aagaiyasur, the demon of fire, doesn't give them fire. But one day, their time will come.

—Tell me about the rebellion.

—About twelve to fourteen years ago, the Bharat *sarkar* sent people to search for iron ore in Lohri. The villagers of Kubha were trouble-making Aagariyas. They said—Our three demon gods live in that hillock. Don't dig that up. Two Punjabi officers, a Madrasi geologist, why would they believe in these *junglee* tales of *asur deotas?* They *blasted* the hillock flat.

—Then?

—The Aagariyas of Kubha attacked and cut down everyone. Then they vanished into the jungle.

—Into the jungle?

—Yes. Once they entered—make note of this, Mr Singh—they entered once and for all, *bas!* They were totally lost. No one ever saw them again. One hundred to one hundred and fifty people.

—What are you saying?

—That's the amazing thing.

—What, without a trace?

—Without a trace! No news of them!

—Didn't the *gorment* try to find them?

—They combed the jungle like a Brahmin widow picks worms from rice.

—Even then they weren't found?

—No.

—After that?

—The *gorment* searched high and low. No one had disappeared from any village other than Kubha. This proved that no one else was guilty. For a month, the search went on. Then the police burnt Kubha village to ashes, sprinkled salt on the earth where it had once stood, and left; punitive taxes were imposed on all other Aagariya villages. A lot of oppression.

—They were never found?

—No.

—Where did they go?

—To the jungle. There are so many hillocks and caves in the jungle—who can say where they went?

—All in Lohri?

—Yes.

—Why do you carry a gun?

—It's scary. So many, many people. Where are they hiding? Suppose they come out?

—That's why?

—No.

—Then?

—Whenever *relief* is sent, it gets stolen. Earlier, four or five sacks would go. For the past few years now, it's

been two or three. A terrible place. Who knows what
there is in that soil! Nothing grows there. My nephew
tried to farm there, once. Nothing grew. Not paddy, not
jowar, not *maroa*, not *bhutta*. Strike the earth with a
plough, and it's as if you hit iron beneath the surface. A
cursed land. You can tell as soon as you set eyes on it.

—The stealing continues?

—Yes. Everyone used to say, little boys and girls steal
the sacks at night. I thought to myself, *relief* material is
usually stolen by those who distribute it. They steal it,
sell it off. The *gorment* knows nothing. Whether it's
winter or summer, they despatch blankets and clothing
as *relief*. What can those *junglee* folk do with Dhariwal
blankets or good clothes or sugar? They'll also just take
it and sell it off, and the *mahajans* will buy it in exchange
for a torch or matches or a mirror. The *relief*-distributors
know this, so they sell it all. I don't think it's wrong.

—But it's not right!

—This kind of not-right stuff happens all the time.
See, at that Bangladesh-war time, the *gorment* sent relief
to Calcutta. Clothes, blankets, mosquito nets, utensils,
stoves, shoes, from all over the world. Didn't we buy it
all in the Ranchi market?

—That's true, too.

—Forget it! I thought, they steal the *relief* themselves
and then make up tall tales about children. So I went
myself, once. Took twenty thousand bucks' worth of
goods with me. I asked for some *sipahis*, too. The camp
was to be at Lohri. Everyone was to come there and pick
up the stuff. But the night was very dark, as dark as the
hair on your head. It was very hot as well. I was sleeping
outside. Suddenly, a strange sound! I got up, and saw
tiny little people—kids, probably—running away with

the sacks.

—What did you do?

—Fired in the air. What could I do! Shoot at kids? But they escaped. They were tiny, naked children! How could I shoot them?

—That's true, too.

—And I thought, so much of the *relief* is stolen, so many people make profit off it, let the kids take some.

—Quite right!

—But . . .

—What?

The BDO knit his brows and stared into the darkness for a while. An extremely hot, airless darkness. A darkness which drips down and clogs all the holes and pores in this world. The dust from the earth, and the steamy air, are cloying. Even the stars in the sky don't sparkle. The moon will rise late at night.

The BDO said—I didn't tell anyone about it. But you're a good man, your maternal uncle is a State Minister. I've never told anyone what I'm going to tell you now. I'll tell you, and I'll also show how to tackle the problem.

—What is it?

—You know, Mr Singh, that place is notorious. People say it's haunted by *asur-bonga*-ghosts. Those little ones fleeing with the sacks were not like human children.

—What do you mean?

—Their limbs were different.

—How?

—I can't say how. What long hair they had! And how they cackled as they vanished into thin air!

—I'm scared.

—You have nothing to fear. I wanted to warn you, so I didn't go to Tahar today. I stayed behind. Your aunt's husband is a State Minister. I take total responsibility for your life. I've brought this *prasad* blessed by Mahabirji. Keep it in your pocket. Whoever has this with him has nothing to fear.

—I don't have a gun, though.

—So what? You'll have people with you.

—Gun-bearing *sipahis* or policemen . . .

—There's no way of requisitioning them now . . . All right. You're going tomorrow. I'll try to send some policemen with the next lot of people who go.

—Come, let's eat.

—Have a bath first.

A bath in cool well water. His aunt's husband—a Minister. Hence, top quality rice served at table. Peas pulao. Meat, *gulabjamun*, pickle.

At night, beds out in the open. The earth dampened with water, so slightly cool.

But how can one sleep? A battle between the sun and a boy. A hillock. Exploding through the darkness, a rebellion. Corpses. Widow. Like a Brahmin widow picking out weevils from rice, the police comb the jungle. *Relief.* In the dark, superhuman children steal rice. Image after image, in procession. When he felt the heat on his face, the *relief officer* realized that he had slept deeply. Undisturbed. Now the rays of the sun were falling on his face.

In the morning, the *relief officer* set out. The BDO returned to Tahar. *Relief* material was loaded in the truck. Including tents.

After a while, the road was unmetalled. One could travel along it because it was summer. In the monsoons, the road was impossible. On the way, he saw that *missionaries* had opened *relief-centres* at *mission houses.* Crowds of people. Dark, emaciated, silent.

The jeep driver spat and said—Animals, all of them. When there's a famine, they dump their kids at the mission gate. They say, Those people won't abandon them. Somehow they'll keep them alive. If they stay with us, they'll die.

—They're inhuman.

—The sahebs of the mission are turning them into Christians, destroying their religion. But they're also a cunning lot. They're turning Christian, but they're worshipping their own gods as well.

—Don't the *missionaries* know?

—They know. But still, they give them medicines, look after them. The white *mems* take these animals' children on their laps. Kiss their lips.

—*Ram Ram.*

—Listen to them sing! Would any civilized person sing like this at such a time?

The long ghostly wails that pass for song now ooze out of all the hillocks and jungles and smatter against the speeding jeep.

—Why are they singing?

—They're like that! Those who can walk will come to take *relief.* Those who can't, those who're too old, will sit in a circle, and sing like that. They'll sing and sing till they die. When the singing starts in one village, the dying old women from the other villages send the youngsters off to collect relief and start keening, themselves.

The *relief officer* begins to drown in a bottomless ocean. In Ranchi, amidst sparkling lights, taxis and cars,

I dreamt about vultures sitting on a fence last night.

life continues. And where is he headed? To a land where supernatural children offer ghostly smiles in reply to gunshots, as they run away with *relief* goods. A land on the road to which you can only see shadowy hills and jungles. In the midst of which, old women do not struggle to survive, even when they know death to be nigh. Where they keen like the wailing of ghosts.

—Do many die?

—Many! See the kites and vultures circling overhead? The vultures devour even living bodies. This is a bizarre land.

—How far is Lohri?

—We're entering it now. See what the trees–land–hills are like! As red as if they're made of copper. This is Lohri. There's poison in the earth here.

A few hills could be seen in the distance. The driver said—That's where your camp will be.

After a while, the driver said again—One thing *hujoor*, don't take it wrong. I don't know what it is about Lohri, but it fills the heart with fear. We'll drink a little *daru-uru* at night. Close to the camp. Otherwise, it gets scary. That Bahadur even went crazy.

—Which Bahadur?

—The driver. Why? Hasn't the *officer* saheb told you about him?

—No.

—He should have.

—What happened to Bahadur?

—We still don't know. Those who were with him say, they were all asleep that night. Bahadur suddenly took off, yelling, Thief! thief! and then disappeared into the dark. Those who went to look for him heard someone laugh in the darkness, got scared, and came back. Next

repetition

Murmansk dream

morning they saw Bahadur lying senseless. He revived, but didn't return to his senses.

—Then?

—Went crazy. He's still insane. He's in Ranchi. Here, we've reached Lohri.

The camp site had been cleared. The *tehsildar* emerged from a small hut. Said—Tea, *hujoor?* Water's ready, you can have a bath, too. Water has to be brought from half a mile away.

The driver said—The same pond?

—The very same.

In reply to the *relief officer's* questioning glance, the *tehsildar* said, After the rebellion at Kubha village, the hillock was *blasted* out of existence, a deep hole left in its place. Water collects there in the monsoon, lasts all year long. That's where the water is from.

After tea, the *tehsildar* puts up the tent. Arranges the *relief* goods, counting the sacks. Says—Don't worry about a thing. I do this every year. We have a list of villagers ready. Distribution is from ten to four, then the game's over.

—How many people will come?

—A thousand, two thousand, nothing fixed.

—A medical unit's coming.

—Here?

—Yes. We'll need tents. So pitch tents.

—Very good, *hujoor.* A medical unit, here?

Never before has there been a *janta sarkar,* nor a *special officer* to distribute *relief.*

To himself the *tehsildar* says—Son of a bitch—and aloud—We'll do as you say.

—Those who have come from Sardoha mission will work here, as well.

—Those people, too?

—Yes. They have a nurse, a doctor.

—Very good.

—We need people to carry water for the camp, to clean up, to wash the vats in which the *khhichri* will be cooked. Go and select ten village boys. Write down their names. They'll all get work, food, and one rupee as daily wages.

—They'll work for food alone.

—Are you here to talk, or to listen? I'm running this camp. You will attend every day.

—How long will the camp function?

—This time, for a month. I'll look after this one. Camps are being set up at twenty-mile intervals. And one more thing. I'll stay in the tent in which the *stores* are kept. It's my responsibility, after all!

—That's very true. I won't stay in the *store* tent even if I'm paid a hundred bucks.

—Why?

—Things get stolen. And those who do the stealing are not human.

—Forget all that. There are college students coming as volunteers, too. Tell everyone, there's no need for the old people to send song messages from village to village. *Relief* will go to the villages. The boys will take it.

Astounded, the *tehsildar* leaves. Every year, he steals from the *relief* and consolidates his own affairs. He is extremely corrupt, but very efficient. He appoints ten Aagariya village youths to clean and look after the camp. The *chowkidar* takes two of them and arranges the relief goods under the trees. Only the dry goods are distributed that day. From the next day, *khhichri* and children's milk will be distributed.

He tells the *relief officer*—These boys will guard the *store* tent. None of us is willing to stay there—will you stay there alone?

The *relief officer* is relieved. Very soon, a disciplined camp is running smoothly. From the next day, *khhichri* is cooked and distributed. The medical unit gives injections against cholera and typhoid. The place becomes a bustling centre.

Now, people begin to come from afar. Even at night, one can see the moving lights on the far horizon. People travel by the light of flaming torches, because the scorching day temperatures make it easier to travel at night. In a few days, even the *tehsildar* says—*Hujoor*, you've restored faith in the hearts of these animals, the way you've been working. Earlier, the old people knew they would die, so they'd begin to sing. Now, the songs are silenced. Why don't we do one thing?

—What?

—Don't send *relief* to the villages. This time they're getting *relief* properly. Let them carry their old people here.

—No, no. Hunger makes people lose all compassion. Whoever isn't brought here will die. And how will they carry them here? They themselves are falling dead by the wayside, trying to get here. They don't have the strength.

The *relief officer* gets completely involved in this *relief* work. The scorched-earth-like appearance of the area, its stunted, dusty and leafless jungles, its reddish, cruel hills, all seem to lose their harshness. The hungry, starving people become *top priority*. The medical team vaccinates people and leaves. He inspires confidence in the minds of the mission doctors and nurses, and even though the regulations allow only cholera and typhoid injections, he supercedes *protocol* and sends for large quantities of antibiotics, medicines for wounds, baby food, *Nutrinuggets* etc. from Ranchi.

The ten village Aagariya boys stay close to him. They don't take him to the blasted-hillock pond. For them, that place is *taboo*. The secret pond in the heart of Lohri river is their own source of water—they take him there. While bathing, he hears from them the legend of the battle between the sun and Jwalamukhi. Jwalamukhi, an Aagariya youth, is their *hero*. He is the reason for the Aagariyas' poverty. On the other hand, it is because of his curse that the sun god cannot mate with his wife except on a full moon night. The three demons, Lohasur, Aagaiyasur and Koilasur, have not blessed them, so the Aagariya are going through hard times now. When he returns after his bath, night has fallen.

He places his bed before the store tent at night, lies down and thinks, they themselves used to steal relief goods hand over fist, which was why they spread tales about thieving spirits. He also wonders whether it will be possible to change their future. Honest and compassionate officers are needed. Such officers will be able to *convert* these people to agriculture. He decides to submit a *note* the moment he gets to Ranchi. It's not possible for so many people to survive only on relief year after year. Thinking these thoughts, he falls asleep. Untroubled sleep. The Aagariya youth sleep around the tent. They have been calling him *deota*—god. When he thinks of this, it seems like a major victory for him. To hear the word *deota* from the mouths of those who do not trust anyone but themselves, is a victory indeed.

The ten youths, though, do not fall asleep. They stay

awake, their ears pricked up. This time, the camp is much larger. There is a lot more bustle—is that the reason?

One night they hear the sound of many footsteps. Many pairs of feet advance, padding forward with canine caution. Muffled whistles. Another whistle in reply. Someone undoes the tent cords. Then swift and silent *activity*. The youths arise and hold up the tent flap. The waning moon in the depths of the night. Sacks of rice are removed, then sacks of milo. Tiny hands.

In a trice, the *relief officer* is wide awake. He sits up and, switching on his torch, sees at once that the Aagariya boys are not there. He goes to the other end of the tent with hasty steps. He sees them securing the tent rope to the pole. Why? Why had the tent flap been opened? Befuddled and wounded with the realization of trust betrayed, he looks at them. Unfamiliar, unknown faces. Those same boys. But in their faces, there is no echo of the despairing question that rends his heart. Smiling the cruel smiles of the victorious, they disappear into the darkness of the forest in the wink of an eye. The *officer* runs round the tent and enters. Two sacks are missing.

He comes out and begins to run. Patter of tiny feet. The sacks are fleeing swiftly through the forest. Not spirits, humans. So small that they may be children. Must be little boys and girls. These people—they take *relief* on the one hand and on the other, force eight- and ten-year-olds to steal. But according to government records, the Lohri Aagariya know nothing of theft–banditry–robbery. They never lie. He had wanted to do them some good. The boys had called him *deota*. Was it all deception? It feels as if someone has robbed him and left him totally bankrupt! Blood rushes to the *relief officer's* brain. He is a good man, honest, doesn't take bribes. He has compassion for the adivasis. These were the reasons for his selection and he had honoured the trust. He had poured his heart and soul into *relief* work. Instead of keeping them alive on once-a-year *relief,* he had even thought of ways to improve their lives on a permanent basis. And this was their behaviour in return? Sending youngsters to steal *relief* goods? He decides to catch them, get to the bottom of this theft before he leaves.

Stubbornly, he continues to run. They also run. The forest thins out. Dry straw-like grass jungles. Fallow land. This is the place where the sun and Jwalamukhi fought. Reaching there, the youths put down the sacks of rice and milo.

They must be exhausted. The *relief officer* goes close, close to the sacks. They stand in a circle around the sacks. Like crouching animals. Violence in their stance. As if they'll spring any moment. Unmoving, silent, marking his every move. All dimly outlined in the faint moonlight.

All at once, they approach him. Not just males, there are females too. Sudden fear paws his heart. Fear, terrible fear. Coming steadily forward, they surround him. Why have they stopped?

They look at him, he at them. They come a little closer. Stop once more. The *relief officer* turns and looks. The circle is closed. No chance of escape. He won't try to escape. Why should he? These are the human children of human beings. Not ghosts, ghosts don't steal rice and milo. 'A cursed land'—who had said that? 'We'll drink some *daru-uru*'—who had said that? The *relief officer* controls his thumping, thundering heart. They come forward.

Fear, terrible fear. Terrible, terrible fear. He feels a terrible fear. Why are they advancing in silence? Why don't they speak? Their bodies are now clearly visible. What's this? Why are they naked? Why is their hair so long? If they are young, young boys, adolescents, then why is their hair white? Why do the girls, the little girls, have empty, sagging breasts? Why is he coming forward? The one with grey hair? Don't come near me—his terrified scream is silenced, what he gasps is—Don't come closer! The grey-haired one, what is he showing, close up? Grotesque, grotesque sight, he holds up his penis, dry, shrivelled, wrinkled.

Not children, *adults!* No sound escapes the *relief officer's* lips. But the impact of realization explodes like Hiroshima–Nagasaki in his mind.

The old man sees that he has realized. He begins to laugh *khik-khik-khik*—inhuman laughter. The laughter spreads. Everyone surrounding the *officer* laughs. Laughing, they leap into the air, squat on their haunches. What'll the *officer* do?

—We're not kids. We're the Aagariya of Kubha village. Ku-bha! D'you know it? Have you heard the name 'Kubha'?

—*Na! Na! Na!* The *officer* wants to cover his eyes. His hands are stuck to his sides. His mind torn by a terrible force. The mind won't command the hands to rise. Mahabirji's *prasad* 'in your pocket'—who had said that?

—We protected the sanctity, and honour, of our sacred hillock by cutting you down; and since then, we've been forest-dwellers. No one was able to catch us. Not one policeman or *sipahi,* no one!

The old man laughs. Everyone laughs. *Khik-khik-khik,*
the ghostly laughter spreads.

—*Na! Na! Na!*

—The other Aagariya keep us alive. Continuously
on the run, not being able to eat, most of us are dead
now.

—*Na! Na!*

The circle closes in. They're nearer now.

—Don't come closer!

—Why shouldn't we? All that rice, all that milo, and
you come all this way just for two sacks? Now that you're
here, take a good look. *Hey* Show him, everyone.

Men hold out their penises, women their breasts.

The old man is now very close. His penis brushes
the *officer's* skin. Front and back. Like a cast-off snake
skin. Scratchy and unclean.

—Just fourteen of us left, now, the rest are dead.
Our bodies have shrivelled and shrunk from lack of
food. The men can only piss, they can't get it up any
more. Women can't bear children. So we steal *relief.* We
must eat and grow again, mustn't we?

—*Na! Na! Na!*

—The Aagariya help us. It's because of the revolt at
Kubha that we're in this state. The revolt at Kubha!

—*Na! Na!* This can't be.

Because if this is true, then all else is false. The
universe according to Copernicus, science, this century,
this freedom, plan after plan. So the *relief officer*
reiterates—*Na! Na! Na!*

—Just saying *Na* won't change things. How else did
we get these? Can't you tell that we're not kids?

They cackle in ghoulish, vengeful glee. Then they
circle him, laughing. Their penises rub against him,

reminders that they are men, adult, Indian males.

The moon overhead. How hopeless the moon looks. How feeble the moonlight. In the wasteland burnt by Jwalamukhi's battle with the sun, the terrible glee of a few adult children. The glee of revenge realized. The glee of hacking off the enemy's head in revolt.

Counter-violence, revenge.

Against what?

Spreading across their dancing silhouettes, his shadow shows against what.

Against his 5-foot 9-inch being.

Against the natural growth of his body.

The logical arguments *motor-race* through the *relief officer's* mind. He wants to say, why this revenge? I'm just an ordinary Indian. Not as well-developed or tall as the Russians–Canadians–Americans. I've never eaten the kind of calorie-rich food required for the development of a strong human body, the failure to consume which is construed as a crime by the World Health Organization.

He can't say a word. Standing under the moon, looking at them, hearing their laughter, feeling their penises on his skin, the undernourished body and laughable height of the ordinary Indian male appear a heinous crime of civilization. He feels like a criminal condemned to death. Pronouncing his own death-sentence for their stunted forms, he lifts his face up to the moon, his mouth gaping wide. They dance, they laugh, scaly penises brushing against him, his only liberation lies in going mad, rending the atmosphere with the howl of a demented dog. But why isn't his brain sending the order for this throat-shattering scream?

Tears stream from his eyes.

seeds

reminds me of Anil's Ghost ~Ondaatje

THE LAND NORTH of Kuruda and Hesadi villages is uneven, arid, sun-baked. Grass doesn't grow here even after the rains. The occasional raised serpent hoods of cactus plants, a few *neem* trees. In the middle of this scorched wasteland where no cattle graze is a low-lying boat-shaped piece of land. Around half a *bigha.* You can spot the land only if you climb a high embankment, and the splash of green appears eerie.

Even more eerie is the *machaan* in the middle of the field, a platform on wooden posts with a thatched hut on it. A hut on this land is most unsettling. For the viewer. Because such a hut is generally built to guard crops. Here there are only stray aloe plants, leaves thorny like the pineapple. Even buffaloes don't eat them. Elsewhere in the world, the fibre from these plants make extremely strong ropes. In India, they are dismissed as wild bushes.

The most eerie scene occurs as evening falls. A man comes striding along from Kuruda village. As he approaches, you can see that he's old, his skin gnarled and knotted, a loincloth wrapped around his waist, from which a quilt bag hangs. He carries a stick and raps the aloe bark at random as he approaches the *machaan*. He climbs the rickety ladder lashed together from tree branches. He strikes a flintstone, lights a *beedi*, and sits on the *machaan*. Every day. When night falls, he spreads a mat and goes to sleep. Every day.

Every day, in Kuruda village, the old wife of Dulan Ganju yells curses at him at this time. This is her right. Because this old man's name is Dulan Ganju. Her son–daughter-in-law–grandchildren dislike this yelling and cursing, but can't do anything about it. If they protest, they'll be abused, too. And Dhatua's mother's abusive powers are legendary in these parts. In every dispute, she is called upon to exhibit her professional squabbling abilities. She takes the field and starts by cursing the first of the adversary's seven previous generations. Generally, by the time she reaches the third generation, the opposition flees the field.

Everyone respects her. When there was trouble at Tamadih during the Emergency, the police had come to this village asking questions. Dhatua's mother's fiery tongue forced them to leave the village. One of the fugitives the police was seeking was hiding in the cowshed loft. Dhatua's mother's strident commands to Come, search every room, you vultures! conclusively prove that the whole village is completely innocent.

But she doesn't stop there. She says—Look, only the children and the elderly are in the village. Want to examine them? Want to arrest them?

Once the police leave, Dhatua's mother bloodies the fugitive with her sharp tongue—Rotoni! You've always been a half-wit! Less sense than an old nanny goat! So you hacked at a Rajput *mahajan* with an axe, excellent, well done. You should've despatched the devil by giving it to him in the neck. Why didn't you hide in the jungle? Which idiot returns to the village? Go, go to the forest!

Dhatua and Latua don't have the guts to tell their mother—Don't curse our *Baap.*

If they do, Ma will explode. So, the old man is now his sons' darling, and their mother a worthless old she-goat! Do the sons know their father's true character? Only she knows.

Ma was married at four. At fourteen, after the *gaona*, she came to make her home with her husband's family. Ma knows that old man through and through. Lord of a thorny wasteland, guarding his land alone. After all, who will be widowed if a snake bites him or a tiger drags him off? Dhatua and Latua? Can they fool the government into giving them seeds every year for that barren land? Collect *sarkari* fertilizer and sell it off? Extract money for a plough and buffalo by displaying the *pahaan's* plough and buffalo, year after year?

The sons fall silent. Ma puffs away at her hookah and, delivering her final, unanswerable line—You'll never know my true worth till I'm dead—goes off to sleep. The daughters-in-law whisper to the sons—Well, another day gone.

Ma addresses the darkness—One day he'll lie there dead. I won't even be there.

The sons know it is totally abnormal to guard the aloe plants every night. But they don't consider their father a normal person by any standards. Baba is a dark character, complicated and incomprehensible. The Ganjus' caste trade is skinning dead animals. Baba once arsenic-poisoned a few buffaloes belonging to the powerful Rajput *mahajan*, Lachman Singh, owner of ten rifles. This in Lachman Singh's own village, Tamadih. Then he sold off the skins. Characteristically, Lachman Singh suspects his brother and co-heir Daitari Singh. The resultant family feud is still raging.

Despite this, Baba survives, proving that he is a man of a different measure. Always busy with such strategies of survival, he has never had time for his sons or grandsons.

Ma is no less. Ma's ripe old bones have such stamina, such stubborn courage and anger, that she, too, is beyond the ordinary measure of a human being.

They have never seen their father and mother sitting together and having a chat. But when Baba is planning something important, he asks Ma to come and sit in the courtyard. Lights her hookah and says—*Eh Dhatua ke ma!* Give me advice. Everyone in the village consults you, even the police are scared of you.

—What mischief are you brewing now? Who're you planning to cheat or rob?

Ma's voice is loud, but without rancour. Together they plot and plan in low voices. Such an event occurs every year or year-and-a-half.

At other times, Baba doesn't pay any attention to Ma. She says—I might as well go back to my father's house.

Baba smiles slyly and quietly tells the breeze—Yes. To that huge mansion of your father's, in Tura village.

Ma has no father–mother–brothers. Yet she gives

Baba the opportunity to smile crookedly and pass mocking remarks.

This is what Latua and Dhatua's parents are like—and there's nothing to be done about it. Just as you can't help the fact that the hill lies to the west, or that Kuruda river flows nearby. Sanichari says—Your father and mother are both mad. Your father, of course, is totally crazy. Why else would he guard that land without ever farming it? Why?

There's a proverb which says that what you pick up free is worth fourteen annas. The land was free, but there wasn't even fourteen paise profit from it.

The land belongs to the abovementioned Lachman Singh. Quite a few years ago, Sarvodaya activists went from door to door to every landlord in this area. About them too, Sanichari used to say—These are madmen of the babu caste. They'll make the landlords remorseful. The landlords will spontaneously say—Tch, tch! We have so much land, and they have none at all? And they'll give away the land. The day they do this, I'll sit on a *chauki*, eat butter and cream, cook rice twice a day.

But the landlords did begin to give away little bits of infertile–stony–barren land to provoke their fellow landlords into doing the same. Everyone has five hundred–seven hundred–a thousand–two thousand *bighas* of fertile land. Everyone harvests paddy–corncobs–maize–*maroa*–mustard–*arhar*. Groundnuts are earning large profits. So it doesn't really matter much if you give away some infertile land.

Gifting land serves many useful purposes. The land is gifted. The Sarvodaya leaders and workers had become the butt of the *Bharatvasis'* mockery. This helped them to save face. Didn't the Rajput–Kayastha,

jotedar–mahajan of the Kuruda belt give up their land?
Doesn't that mean they've had a change of heart?
Certainly. *Bas.* The Sarvodayi *mission* is successful.
Immediately after this, they go off to change the hearts
of the dacoits in Madhya Pradesh. Their *mission* won't
be complete until they can fill with remorse the hearts
of two classes—the landlords and the dacoits.

This gifting of land has many uses. Barren land can
be got rid of. The recipients are bought over. One's
position with the *sarkar* becomes stronger. Above all,
like a *rossogolla* after a meal, there is the added
satisfaction of knowing one is compassionate.

Dulan Ganju gets this land. He didn't want to take
it. But Lachman Singh is too powerful. His eyes grew
red with anger and he said—Typical of you lowcastes!
Today I'm feeling generous, so I'm giving you this. Fool,
do you think I'll feel this way tomorrow?

Dulan said—*Hujoor* is my *ma-baap.*

—Then? Low-lying land, flooded by water every
monsoon, sow whatever you like, and you'll get high
yields.

During the monsoons, reddish water streams down
the embankment and collects in the field. But there is
barren, stony ground on all sides. Who'll go all that way
to plough that land? If it was fertile land, would
Lachman Singh have let it lie fallow? Dulan had gone to
borrow money. He came back a landlord.

Everyone in the village said—It's a rich man's whim!
He eats *parathas* soaked in *ghee,* and the heat's gone to
his head. He'll forget all about it tomorrow.

—Suppose he doesn't?

—Just let the land be. In Ara–Chhapra, this is the
kind of land they gave at the behest of the Sarvodayis.

Those who got it sold it back to the *mahajan* or mortgaged it to him. You'll do the same.

—Who'll take that land? The *mahajan's* buying himself a good name, and at the same time getting rid of it.

Dulan would have said more, but the *pahaan* gave him a mighty tongue-lashing. They have so many problems. Dulan's land trouble is nothing in comparison.

Dulan mutters and grumbles.

His wife says—Oh! He's busy calculating how to make a profit from this land, but just look at the fuss he's making! No one's ever wised up to his wiles.

Profit from this land?

The next day, Sanichari hears all about it and says— Why? *Eh, Dhatua ke maiya!* If he gets land, *Dhatua ke baap* can go to Tohri! To the BD office! The *sarkar* will bear the expenses of farming, seeds, everything!

Only when he heard this did Dulan smile. His eyes glazed over with dreams.

In some fairy tales, cows yield milk though they aren't pregnant. Even a person like Dulan had not realized how barren land could help him to run his household.

One day, the land came into Dulan's possession in the form of documents and deeds. They had two adjacent rooms and a corridor in the Ganju neighbourhood: rooms that served as living room, kitchen, everything. This was his world. Barricaded, one end of the corridor turned into a bedroom for husband and wife. Someone so bereft of support generally has no backbone. All around him are Rajput *jotedars* and *mahajans,* the Brahmin priest Hanuman Misra of Tahar is particularly influential in these parts. Living in such an area, continuously under the thumb of the higher castes, it was only natural for Dulan's spirit to be broken.

But the drive for survival prompts him to exploit situations by using his natural guile rather than force. He fools his powerful adversaries not by strength, but by wit and cunning, and all the stratagems of survival are at his fingertips.

Dhatua's mother says—It's a large piece of land, very fertile. Oh, Dhatua, tell your *baap* to build a granary for his crops. Oh, Latua *re*, your father's become a *zamindar*, yes, a *zamindar*!

She said all this, but the villagers and she continued to wait. To see what Dulan would do.

The villagers are appreciative witnesses to Dulan's single-handed strategic warfare. Everyone knew about the business of Lachman Singh's buffaloes, but no one told on Dulan. He sells a pumpkin to Daitari Singh's household and takes money from both Daitari's wife, and mother. When the banana-radish-vegetables-fruits are brought in a bullock cart from Lachman Singh's house to the banks of the Kuruda river during the Chhatt festival, he walks beside the cart, shooing away imaginary birds, and continuously lifts things. He has never given a single thing to the other villagers. Yet, they treat him with respect. He can do what they can't.

As soon as he got the land, Dulan touched Lachman Singh's knees and said—*Malik*, protector! You've given me land, but how will I farm it? I won't get a thing from the BD office. *Ahaha*, such a good piece of land! I've got it but I can't use it.

—Why? The BD office will give you everything.

—No *hujoor*, I'm a lowcaste.

—Of course you are. It's because you don't remember this that you get kicked around. Sure, you're a lowcaste! But how can they refuse to help someone I'm giving land to? Who's the BD babu?

—Kayasth, *hujoor*. Says the Rajputs are stupid country bumpkins. Listens to the radio all the time and uses his left hand to drink water, tea.

—*Arrey Ram Ram*! *Chhee, chhee, chhee.*

—I've seen it myself, *hujoor*.

—I'll write to him.

Lachman Singh is no learned *mahapundit*. He keeps a *vakil*. The *vakil* writes a strong appeal in *kayathi* Hindi advocating that Dulan get money in instalments to buy a plough and bullocks, seed and fertilizer. The BDO might live in Tohri, and it's true that Tohri is far from Lachman's village Tamadih, but he has only one life. The SDO himself has warned him about not getting into conflict with Lachman and Hanuman Misra.

He immediately agreed to everything. He explained to the loincloth-clad Dulan in a very gentle voice that he would get seeds, and fertilizer. But he wouldn't get the entire amount for the plough and bullock at one go. If he can pay an advance and show that he's bought the plough and bullock, he'll get the rest of the money.

Dulan returned to the village and said to the *pahaan*—The *sarkar* makes laws, but doesn't understand anything. People buy ploughs and bullocks with cash. Who will sell to someone who pays in instalments? Lend me your plough and bullock.

Dulan got the money by displaying that plough and bullock. Every alternate year. Every time he takes the money, he says, the bullock died, *hujoor*.

He takes the money. Collects the fertilizer and sells
it at Tohri itself. Hoists the sack of seeds onto his
shoulder and brings it home.

He eats the seeds.

It's no easy task to boil the paddy seeds and make
rice. But he does it. The first time, his wife had said—So
much seed! How much land do you have?

—You can't measure it even if you try.

—What do you mean?

—Our hunger. Can hunger be measured? The land
of one's stomach keeps increasing! You want me to farm
that barren strip of land? Are you crazy?

—What'll you do, then?

—Boil it, grind it, we'll eat it.

—Are you going to kill yourself eating seeds?

—We haven't died yet. Didn't we eat rats during the
famine? Why should we die from eating seeds? If we do,
at least we'll have died eating rice! We'll go to heaven.

It took Dhatua's mother just one meal of rice made
from the seeds to realize that she had never eaten
anything so sweet in her life.

She proudly told everyone in the village about this
tasty food. Can any other married woman in the village
boast of how brainy her man is, of how cunningly he
fools the *gorment* so that his family can eat rice made
from paddy seeds?

Everyone in the village was pleased. The *gorment* has
never protected their interests. The *gorment's* BDO never
helps them with farming. Their children never get to
enter the *gorment's* primary school. Lachman Singh or
Daitari Singh force them to harvest their crops for four
annas a day or one meal, at gun point. There is a lot of
tension over this, because the Ganju–Dushad–Dhobis of

the neighbouring block are getting kicked and fed for
eight annas daily. The villagers want a raise of twenty-
five paise. Knowing all this, whenever there's trouble,
the SDO brings the police and picks up the labourers.
Lachman Singh or Daitari are let off without a word.

The *gorment* belongs to Lachman Singh. The *gorment*
belongs to Lachman Singh, Daitari Singh, Hanuman
Misra. If such a *gorment* is fleeced by someone who
happens to be a Dulan Ganju, then the villagers are
bound to be full of appreciation.

Like Kaamdhenu, the land continued to gift Dulan
about six hundred rupees annually. But Dulan
continued to sleep indoors. At the corner of the
covered verandah, on a platform, beside Dhatua's
mother. Dhatua's mother coughs and has asthma. They
tie a billy goat beneath the platform when they go to
sleep. One son per room, each with his wife and
children. Wheat-*maroa*-corn cobs by the sackful, pots
and pans, firewood, everything stacked in the same
rooms. The earnings from the land don't see them
through the whole year. Then, father and sons work as
field labourers, go to the forest in search of wild
potatoes, carry loads in Tohri. Work in Misraji's
orchards. Like everyone else.

One day Karan Dushad of Tamadih arrived in the
village. A glamorous personality. Used to work as a
labourer in Lachman's field. He had a dispute over
wages with the *malik* protector, and went to jail. In jail,
at Hazaribagh, he made friends with prisoners from
other parts of Bihar.

They didn't shrink from him because he was a
'Dushad'. They respected him as a fighter. They were
amazed that without the help of any organization, two

hundred field labourers had turned against an ocean of exploitation and set fire to the ripe wheat owned by the powerful Lachman Singh. They explain to him the importance of battles like theirs burgeoning all over. The need for getting organized to fight. Fighting from one's own base.

They are tortured, go on hunger strike. Get beaten up by the authorities. So many are beaten to death. Even after all this, they tell Karan—You're a fighter, you did the right thing, never give up the fight.

Hence, there is turmoil in the layers of Karan Dushad's mind. The Karan who had rebelled only when Lachman Singh had driven him to the end of his tether, now came out of jail and said to everyone—Conditions are unchanged. Why wait till he forces us to resist, get shot at, get jailed? Let's organize ourselves in advance. Talk things over with him. Ask the police to be present during harvesting. Our demands are very few. We're harijans and adivasis. We won't get good wages in these parts. We'll fight for eight annas. Women–men–children, eight annas for everyone. He's giving four annas. This will be our 'twenty-five paise battle' for an additional four annas.

As soon as Dulan hears this, he calls Karan to Kuruda. He is suspicious by nature. They talk on the embankment at the edge of Dulan's land, away from everyone. Karan Dushad is middle-aged, thin, a tiny man. After two years with the prisoners in Hazaribagh, he is like a new person.

—All this caste business is rubbish. It's the Brahmin and the wealthy who have spun these tales about untouchability.

His words startle Dulan. For a moment he is

speechless. Then—he's an old fox, after all! says—Oh,
the babus who can read and write always say that. Now
let's get down to business. That Lachman Singh and the
BDO, SDO and *daroga* are drinking mates. First go to
the Adivasi Office and the Harijan Seva Sangh at Tohri.
Keep them informed. Let them go with you to the *thana*
and the SDO.

—Why? Are we that weak?

—Yes, we are, Karan. Make no mistake. The entire
sarkar will help Lachman. He can open fire and they
won't notice. But you raise a stick and they'll catch you.
Madanlalji of the Harijan Seva Sangh is a good man.
Everyone knows him. Keep him on your side.

Karan takes this advice. Madanlal can garner a
powerful pool of votes. So the SDO and *daroga* first hold
a secret meeting with Lachman Singh. Then they agree
to what Madanlal says.

The harvesting and gathering of the corn went off
without incident. Eight annas as wages. Karan Dushad
became a *hero*. A fairy tale come true.

Then, abruptly, Lachman says to Dulan—Stay on
your land tomorrow. If anyone gets to know that I've
told you this, I'll kill you.

When this 'tomorrow' turns into 'today' at daybreak,
the SDO suddenly goes off to Ranchi and the *daroga* to
far-off Purudiha, chasing bandits.

As evening draws to dusk, in the radiance of the
setting sun, Lachman Singh, accompanied by his Rajput
caste-brothers, attacks the Dushad quarters in Tamadih.

Fires rage, people burn, huts collapse.

At night, the newly risen moon reveals an unearthly,
silent scene before Dulan's eyes. Lachman Singh on
horseback. Two horses tied abreast, a plank across their

backs, laden with corpses. Ten of Lachman's men.

At the point of Lachman's gun, Dulan buries Karan and his peaceable brother Bulaki in his land. Terrified, head bowed, he digs deep holes with his shovel. Lachman stands on the edge of the field, supervising and chewing *paan*. Then he says—Breathe a word of this to anyone, you cur, and you'll join Karan Dushad. We can't trust the jackals and wolves not to dig up the corpses. Build a *machaan* here tomorrow. Stay on guard at night. I'm the son of a Rajput! Karan lit this fire— from now on, there'll be more dead bodies. Dulan nods. In order to survive, he says—As you wish.

The police come the next day. A lot of hullabaloo. Ultimately it is learnt that Karan wasn't even present during the event; reporters' attempts to write 'A True Harijan Story' at all costs are totally foiled. No one says a word against Lachman Singh. One of his henchmen spends a few days in jail for arson. The government gives a pittance to those rendered homeless, for the construction of new huts.

From then on, Dulan sleeps on the land. At first, this is seen as a sign of insanity, and his sons try to dissuade him. No advice penetrates Dulan's ears at this *stage*. Asked his reasons, he glowers silently at them with bloodshot eyes. Then, shaking his head, he threatens them with his stick—Don't talk to me, Dhatua! I'll break your head.

A great explosion, a landslide, occurs in the strata of his mind, resulting in mental upheaval. So easy! Is everything so easy for the Lachmans? Dulan had thought that just as a man's life is linked to so many rites and rituals, so is his death. But Lachman Singh has proved that these time-honoured customs are meaningless. How easy! Two corpses on horseback! And these corpses must have been carried off arrogantly, from right under the Tamadih Dushads' noses. Lachman knows there's no need to hide them. Those who see won't say anything. They have read the warning in Lachman's sharp, silent gaze. He who opens his mouth will die. This has happened before. Will happen again. Once in a while it is necessary to rend the sky with leaping flames and the screams of the dying, just to remind the harijans and untouchables that government laws, appointment of officers and constitutional decrees are nothing. Rajputs remain Rajputs, Brahmins remain Brahmins and Dushad–Chamar–Ganju–Dhobi remain lower than Brahmin–Kayasth–Rajput–Bhumihar–Kurmi. The Rajput or Brahmin or Kayasth or Bhumihar or Yadav or Kurmi is, in places, as poor as, or even poorer than, the harijan. But they are not tossed into the flames because of their caste. The fire god, having tasted the flesh of forest-dwelling black-skinned outcasts during the burning of Khandav forest, is fond of the taste of the untouchable poor.

All this causes havoc in Dulan's mind. Before this, his was a *surface* cunning. Aimed at survival. Now he has to conceal two corpses beneath his heart. They begin to rot within him. Buried in the earth, Karan and Bulaki grow lighter as they gradually lose the burden of flesh. But in the realm of Dulan's mind, the corpses weigh heavy. He looks wan, hardly speaks. He can't take anyone into confidence. The constant burden he bears makes him feel as if he is tied to a whipping post. If he opens his mouth, the Dushad quarters of Kuruda will go up in flames, ashes flying, the stench of charred flesh.

Slowly time passes. Everyone is forced to forget that
two people, Karan and Bulaki, are missing. From Tohri
to Burudiha on one side and Phuljhar on the other, rail
tracks are laid. According to area and jurisdiction, the
thana and the SDO are given special powers to
immediately investigate, take action, prepare *cases* for
court, in atrocities against adivasis and harijans. A
panchayati well is dug in Dhai village. Dhai is a lower
caste and adivasi village. In this fashion, the area
attempts to limp towards modernity.

The result of all this is to make Lachman Singh
more powerful. He pooh-poohs government dictates
and pays field labourers forty paise as wages, gifts a
golden cobra to crown the Shiva idol in Hanuman
Misra's temple, buys the BDO a scooter and the *daroga* a
transistor, and occupies the *bigha*-and-a-half of land
belonging to Karan and Bulaki as repayment for an old
loan.

The people accept all this. But all at once, there is a
government circular about field labourers and with it
comes a new SDO. This man is suspected of being left-
of-centre, and because it is the administration's pious
intention to drive the final nail into his coffin and
suspend him, he is transferred to Tohri one-and-a -half
months before the harvesting season begins.

The field labourers in the Tohri area are harijans
and adivasis. The landowners, *jotedars* and *mahajans* are
upper caste. The particular problem of the area is the
deep distrust the labourers feel for the masters. This
explains the lack of progress in agriculture or increase
in individual incomes. Income–expenditure–health–
education–social consciousness, everything continues to
remain at a *sub-normal* level. An enlightened,

sympathetic, humane officer is needed here.

The SDO realizes that he's been jacked. He tells his father-in-law—You win. Look for a bank job for me. I'm a student of *Agro-economics*, I might even get it. Or else, where they're sending me, your only daughter will definitely end up a widow.

Having made alternate job arrangements, the SDO tells the impatient field labourers—You have the right to get five rupees eighty paise as wages. He officially informs the *jotedars* of this. Lachman Singh's land and crop and labourers are spread over a vast area, including villages like Tamadih–Burudiha–Kuruda–Hesadi–Chama–Dhai. The son of the Burudiha village headman, Asrafi Mahato, says—We still remember Karan. We haven't forgotten him these three years. But this SDO is a good man. Why should we harvest crops for just forty paise and a meal? Five rupees eighty paise! We don't want the meal, let him give us five rupees forty paise as total wages.

As he had once explained to Karan, so Dulan now carefully explains to Asrafi—Karan raised a ruckus. As a result, Tamadih's Dushad quarters went up in flames.

—Where's Karan? Where's Bulaki?

—Who knows?

—They're dead.

—Why do you say that?

—They've been killed and buried in the jungle.

—I don't know. But keep the *hakim* with you when you act.

—All right.

—Get the *hakim* to help you later, too. That time, they paid the wages. But later, they lit the fire.

—I'll tell him.

In every area, every conflict has a characteristic local *pattern.* Lachman Singh says—I won't pay that much. Just two rupees, and tiffin.

—Give us the wages, *hujoor* protector.

—Should I?

Lachman Singh's eyes are terribly gentle and sympathetic. He says—Let me think about it! You do the same. Even a donkey knows that those wages are fair. But you know what? You mentioned the SDO, right? Go tell him, in these parts, Makhan Singh, Daitari Singh, Ramlagan Singh, Hujuri Prasad Mahato, no one is giving these wages. Why should I alone be ruined? Asrafi offers a timid but stubborn smile—Ruined, *hujoor?* You own the flour mill, your mansion can be seen from miles away—how can you be ruined?

To Lachman Singh this smile is arrogant mockery. He says—The rate I mentioned is what we decided amongst us. Because we own land, the *sarkar* treats us like thieves. Yet you get *sarkari* aid for whatever little land you have. I've given Dulan land. The bastard doesn't farm it, but he collects seeds every year. Animal! He eats them. So let him. And what aid do we get? Fertilizer–seeds–insecticide, we have to buy everything ourselves. Tell the SDO what I said.

Asrafi tells Dulan—Be careful, *chacha!* The bastard knows that you don't farm the land or harvest crops.

The corpses weigh even heavier on Dulan's mind. Lachman Singh has warned him—Don't sow or plough the land for a few years, Dulan.

Dulan, sorrowfully and with deep concern for Asrafi, says—Don't trust him, *beta.* Your father performed the birth rites for my Dhatua-Latua.

—No, *chacha.*

Asrafi keeps shuttling between the SDO and Lachman Singh. Dulan grows increasingly depressed. Fearing some calamity, he growls at his sons—The son of the lowborn will always be lowborn. You eat whatever I manage to wring from the soil. Someone else would have gone off to a nearby colliery. Why are you hanging on here?

Dhatua raises his calm, dreamy eyes and says—This time we'll get double wages, Baba.

Dulan says nothing further. He goes to the Block Office at Tohri, says—This time I want to sow *rabi* after the harvest. I need help.

The BDO seems to know the irrefutable reason for continuing to supply seeds for land that will never be farmed. He, too, joins Lachman and Dulan in this conspiracy and, smiling toothily, says—I'll look into it.

Dulan notices the huge trees in his compound. Such tall papaya trees are rare.

He says—How did this *papita* tree grow so tall, Babu?

The BDO gives a deeply self-satisfied smile—This area became part of the office compound later. During the summer they would shoot mad dogs and dump them in the hole there. Trees are bound to grow well if they're fertilized by rotting bones and flesh.

—Does it make good fertilizer?

—Very good. Haven't you seen how flowers flourish on the burial mounds of poor Muslims?

These words cause the corpses to weigh lighter in Dulan's mind. Returning to his village, Dulan goes to the land in the middle of the afternoon. Yes, true enough! Karan and Bulaki are now those *putush* bushes and aloe plants! Tears strain at his eyes. Karan, you haven't died even in death. But these *putush* bushes and aloe plants are of no use to anybody, even buffaloes and goats don't eat them. You fought for our rights. Why couldn't you turn into corn or wheat? Or, at the very least, china grass? So we could eat *ghato* made of the boiled seeds?

In deep sorrow, he went to Tamadih and, as nobody was around, uprooted and threw away the fence protecting Lachman Singh's vegetable patch. Har–har–har! he called, as he urged a few buffaloes into the kitchen garden. Then he took the roundabout route to the front, entered and said to Lachman Singh—*Malik* protector, write me a letter. I want admission into hospital. Cough and chest pain.

—I'll give you the letter after the harvesting.

—Very good, master.

Once more, the corpses weigh Dulan down. He goes back, digging the depths of his mind with the pickaxe of anxiety. Tells Karan and Bulaki to move over and make space.

—After the harvesting is over! Is someone coming to keep Karan and Bulaki company?

The harvesting is under way. After much debate, two rupees fifty paise a day and a snack are decided upon. Lachman Singh supervises on horseback. The police ceremonially make an appearance and confirm that the harvesting is peaceful. On the seventh day, everyone gets their wages.

Heaving a sigh of relief, the SDO leaves with the police.

On the eighth day, the storm breaks. Lachman Singh brings in outside labourers to harvest the paddy. Asrafi and the others feel threatened, but, though scared, speak up stubbornly.

—You can't do this.

—Who says so? I *am* doing it. Sons of bitches, see for yourself—I can do it.

—But—

—I let you work. I paid you your wages. *Bas*—the game's over!

Seeing Asrafi and the others on the verge of creating trouble, the outsiders lower their scythes and huddle together. Shots are fired. The outside labourers are fleeing, they've gone.

Shots are fired.

There is no account of the number shot dead. According to Dulan and the others, eleven. According to Lachman Singh and the police, seven. Asrafi's father loses his sons. Two sons, Mohar and Asrafi, both missing. Mahuban Kairi of Chama village and Paras Dhobi of Burudiha—missing. Cries of mourning in almost every home. When the SDO comes, the fathers–mothers–wives–children of the dead and missing fall at his feet. The SDO's face is as if hewn from rock. He promises the villagers that he'll file a *police case* against Lachman Singh. He's telling the reporters the whole story, escorting them around. Until the warrant comes, *Lachman Singh is not to leave home.*

And on a moonlit night, when there's a nip in the sweet-scented air, Lachman Singh arrives. Everything in these areas follows a *pattern,* and the noblest animal, the four-footed horse . . . Four horses carrying four corpses. This time, Lachman's men help Dulan. Deep, deep pits are needed. The land is soaked with monsoon rain and autumn dew. Four corpses piled one on the other. The burden within Dulan grows even heavier.

Dulan becomes increasingly strange. He picks

quarrels at the BD Office to extract more and more seeds. Money for a plough and buffalo. Then, before the month is out, a few aloe plants bring solace. Very healthy, very green aloe plants and *putush* bushes accept the salutations of the sun each dawn during the Emergency in neglected southeast Bihar, silent testimony to the murder of field labourers *cum* harijans. Lachman is released without being charged. Emergency. The SDO is demoted for undermining the harmony between the labourers and the landowners by inciting the former to revolt. Lachman and the other *jotedars–mahajans* offer *puja* at Hanuman Misra's temple with savage fanfare and a hundred and eight pure silver *bel* leaves, and announce that only those sons and daughters of curs and bitches who are willing to work for one rupee without food or water, need bother to show up. They can bring in outside labour. The Emergency causes widespread calamity. Congress musclemen have contracted to get outside labourers. Now the game hots up, becomes even more cruelly entertaining. Four annas out of each day's wages have to be given to the contractor. Whether you are contracted by him or not. These musclemen have vowed that they'll get the crop harvested at gun point, and anyone who dares object will be doused in petrol and set on fire, so that matters are settled once and for all.

Dulan wanders around with a heavy mind, and, looking at Dhatua-Latua, wonders if they should flee. But where can they go? Where will a Dulan Ganju be safe in his motherland of southeast Bihar?

Where will there be no Lachman Singhs?

During the Holi festival, he doesn't even listen to the songs carefully. But suddenly the joyous celebrations

are interrupted by a strange song. Dhatua, intoxicated
with *moua*, plays the *tuila* and sings, his eyes closed—

> Where has Karan gone?
> And Bulaki?
> Why is there no news of them?
> They are lost in the police files.
> Where is Asrafi Hajam?
> And his brother Mohar?
> Where are Mahuban and Paras?
> Why is there no news of them?
> They are lost in the police files.
> Karan fought the twenty-five paise battle.
> Asrafi fought the five rupees forty paise battle.
> Bulaki and Mohar
> Fought alongside their elder brothers.
> Mahuban could brew the best *moua*
> Paras was the best Holi dancer
> All lost in the police files, lost.

The song ends. Everyone is silent. The colours of
Holi turn to ash, the intoxication wears off. Dulan
stands up.

—Who made up this song?

—I did, Baba.

Dulan broke into deep sobs. He said—Forget that
song. Or you'll also get lost in the police files.

Dulan returned to his land. Climbed down the
embankment, into the middle. In an eerie whisper he
said—You've become songs. You hear? Songs. Songs
made up by my son Dhatua. You've become *gaan*, song,
not *dhaan*, paddy, not china grass—now get off my
chest, I can't take it any more!

Under the full Holi moon, the fresh leaves of the

aloe plants and the rough-barked *putush* bushes shook
with laughter. They had never heard anything so funny.
Dulan's heart was filled with an unnamed fear for
Dhatua. As soon as he climbed the *machaan*, he heard
Dhatua's song. Now everyone was singing it. But they
were not lost in the police files. Dulan would never be
able to reveal everything. The power of Lachman Singh.
    One day, the Emergency comes to an end.
    One day, the Liberation-Sun of India gets off the
gaddi, her seat of power, to watch the fun, and then,
regaining her breath, a little later, begins agitating to
regain the *gaddi*. One day, Lachman Singh's crop
ripens, once again.
    After two years of drought–famine–crop destruction,
this year the earth generously floods the land with
paddy. Paddy fields disappearing into the horizon,
punctuated with rows of *machaans*. Birds feed on the
ripening paddy day and night.
    He who was a Congressman and muscleman and
field-labour contractor two years ago now expunges the
'Congress and muscleman' *doctorate* from his name and
appears as the Contractor of Field Labour. With him are
a terrylene-and-dark-glasses-flaunting, gun-toting
foursome, all exactly like him. In an Amitabh Bachchan
voice, this *mercenary* tells Lachman Singh—Your days are
over. Now, strike-breaking, supplying contract labour
and harvesting is managed by professionals. I provide
mercenary services in *southeastern* Bihar. This service is
compulsory. Five thousand bucks. Advance.
    —Five thousand?
    —Are you willing to pay the *sarkar's* fixed wage rate?
    —No, no.
    —By not paying those rates, you stand to make a

profit of eighty thousand. And you don't want to pay five thousand?

—I'll pay.

—*Bas.* Give me the names of the villages and the labourers. Any trouble-makers?

—No.

—All right. I have to provide *services* to Ramlagan Singh and Makhan Singh, too. I'll come at the appropriate time. And yes, pay them five *sikka* as wages. My share is four annas.

—One rupee.

—Five *sikka.* Amarnath Misra doesn't waste words.

—How are you related to Misraji of Tahar?

—*Bhatija.* His brother's son. The seed *capital* for my *services* was provided by *chachaji* himself. Thus, everything is settled. Later, Hanuman Misra says to Lachman Singh—Yes, yes, he's my *bhatija.* I bought *surface collieries* for my sons, and asked him, shall I get you one, too? But no, he didn't want such tiresome work. Very competent and efficient. Election candidates use his *services,* as do owners of factories on strike. He supplies *labour* for *surface collieries.* Very efficient! Three wives. Keeps them in different *towns.* Built a house for each one. The previous *sarkar* knew his worth. Not one of my sons turned out as clever as him.

Lachman Singh, a savage Rajput, is all-powerful in his own territory. But even he accepts that when a *mercenary* forces *services* down his throat, he has no choice. Or he'll be pipped at the post by Makhan and Ramlagan.

Harvesting begins. No outside labourers. Dhatua and the others are doing it themselves. A snack of corn *sattu*–chilli–salt and *five sikka* daily wages. Dhatua's mother packs wild *karamcha* pickle for her two sons to take with them.

Dulan sits on the *machaan*. Sits and waits—for what? Harvesting is going on. The women are singing as they reap; from a distance it sounds like a lullaby. But Dulan can't sleep.

> Who has stolen the sleep from Dulan's eyes?
> His sleep is lost in the police files.

Dulan waits at home for Dhatua and Latua to return. Then he goes to his land. In the monsoons, wet with showers and the autumn dew, the aloe plants and bushes stand arrogant, like a rampant jungle. The bushes are bursting with *putush* flowers. Sleep eludes Dulan's eyes.

The expected trouble begins on pay day. Amarnath demands his share. Lachman says—No bloodshed, please. You and I have no agreement about cutting your share from the wages. Settle it with them.

—With all of them? Amarnath laughs like a hyena— You pay me.

Dulan's son Dhatua resists the most. That's why Lachman Singh doesn't want to get involved. The only way he knows of dealing with the untouchable is a bullet from his gun. This is one person he doesn't want to shoot. Dulan is too useful to him.

Amarnath says—Talk to these curs? Five *sikka* for five hundred people. One *sikka* per day per head works out to 1875 rupees for fifteen days. Hand it over.

—No *hujoor*! We won't, Dhatua protests. Lachman sighs. Once again, he will have to work to pattern. Once again he will have to pick up his gun. Karan went, Asrafi came, Asrafi went, now there's Dhatua.

—How can we take home fifteen rupees for fifteen days? Shouldn't we get eighteen rupees twelve annas? Wasn't that agreed upon? We haven't delayed the work, have we?

—Watch it, Dhatua.

Lachman Singh hands the money to Amarnath. Then he says—Don't say a word, Dhatua. Just leave.

Karan was vocal with his demands. Asrafi was aggressive. Dhatua had never known that he could protest so stubbornly over this matter of cutting Amarnath's share from their wages. Stepping out, he tells the others—You carry on. I'll settle things before I leave here.

He returns to face Lachman Singh. Says—If you don't settle the account for the remaining twenty-five paise, we won't come to work tomorrow. The best fields are not yet done. We won't work, and we won't let anyone else work, either.

—You're lucky the police are here for their cut, Dhatua. You're safe this time.

—Why? Do the police scare you?

Dhatua leaves, but this last barb enrages Lachman Singh. Even so, since Dhatua is Dulan's son, and Dulan is necessary to his secret, Lachman Singh gives the lower castes a day's time.

The next day, everyone comes, but no one starts work. Lachman huffs and puffs in frustrated fury. The *mercenaries* are not available. They have gone to help out Makhan Singh and Ramlagan Singh. Outside *labour* is not available at short notice. As the light fades into evening, Lachman gives his men the necessary instructions—If threats do the trick, don't open fire. Lachman's men ride their horses through the ripe paddy. Having seen several films on the Chambal dacoit gangs, they too have donned *khaki* green *uniforms*. They advance. The other side rises and waits.

—Listen here, you whelps, you sons of bitches!

—You're the son of a bitch!

Someone shouts. They raise their guns. This side storms into the fields at amazing speed. They vanish into the paddy. First, verbal *missiles* speed back and forth. Then the inevitable bullets fly. Lots of them. Flocks of birds leave the ripe paddy and take flight. In the field, someone *gargles* blood deep in his throat. A familiar sound.

Then, sharp scythes and iron choppers slash the horses' hooves, keep slashing. The horses and their riders thunder on. The others steal out and flee. Latua and Param run off towards Tohri.

A long, long, agonizing wait for Dulan. Evening turns to night, and the night is far gone when Latua returns.

—Where is Dhatua?

—I haven't seen him. Hasn't he returned? I went to the police *thana.*

—Where is Dhatua?

—We fetched the police. They'll come here as well. The same SDO, Baba. He's back. He'll come too.

—Dhatua!

Why are the corpses stirring deep within Dulan? For whom are they making place? For whom? Realization hits Dulan. He starts up.

—Where are you going?

—To the land.

—The boy is missing, and you . . . you . . . are you mad, or are you a ghoul?

—Shut up, woman.

Dulan walks out, begins to run. Dhatua's song, Dhatua's song,

> Where has Karan gone?
> And Bulaki?
> They are lost in the police files.

Dreamy eyes. A birthmark on his hand. Don't you get lost, now, Dhatua, don't you get lost. Oh, you aloe plant, you *putush* bush, don't you laugh at me tonight.

Dhatua is alive, alive.

Lachman Singh. A man. With bloodied face and eyes. Lachman is hitting him. Kicking him. The man falls to the ground.

Two of them, three horses.

Lachman looks at him. Comes close, says,

—Dulan?

—Dhatua?

—Sorry, Dulan, I forbade them, but still these beasts opened fire.

Lachman kicks the man again. Curses—Trigger-happy tough!

—Dhatua?

—Buried.

—Who buried him?

—This animal.

—Him?

—Yes. But don't open your mouth, Dulan. Or else your wife, son, son's wife, grandson, no one will be spared. Take, I'll give you money, lots of money. Your son called the police. I'll buy them off, of course. But remember that I'm sparing Latua only because he's your son. I haven't fired a single bullet today. I could have felled Dhatua with a single shot. I didn't.

They go away. Dulan can no longer stand there with seven corpses. He falls onto the embankment. Rolls down into the field, torn by the savage leaves and thorns of the aloe plants, till he comes to a halt.

As usual, the investigation remains incomplete. The SDO intervenes. The trigger-happy tough and Amarnath go to jail.

Dhatua does not return.

Dulan ponders, on and on. Finally, he decides to go mad. Because he starts uprooting the aloe and *putush* from his land at the first Baisakhi showers.

—Where's he gone? In the middle of the afternoon? His wife asks. Latua's wife says—Father-in-law took the scythe and the shovel and went to the field.

—Why didn't you stop him?

—Me? Talk to him?!

All grief forgotten, his wife rushes out. She climbs the embankment and yells—Here, have you gone mad? Why are you trying to clear that jungle?

—Go home.

—What do you mean, go home?

—Go home.

In tears, his wife goes to the *pahaan*. The *pahaan* goes to him. Says—Dhatua will come back, Dulan. Don't go crazy in despair over your son. Come, you'll fall ill in the heat of the sun.

Dulan says—Go home, *pahaan*. Is my son missing or is yours?

—Yours.

—Is this my land or yours?

—Yours.

—Well, then? I may be mad or I may not. What's it

to you? I'll fix that *saala's* land!

—Then get Latua to help you.

—No, I'll do it all alone.

Though he doesn't farm, he has green fingers, the *pahaan* remembers. The *pahaan* tells Dulan's wife— Come let's go home. Let him do what he wants. You have to go to Tohri.

Dulan's wife and Latua visit Tohri repeatedly to enquire at the *thana* about Dhatua.

For a few days, Dulan clears the undergrowth. Prepares the land. Then he fetches the seed and says— These seeds are not for eating. I'll sow them on the land.

—On that land!

—Yes.

Scattering seeds on the land, he chants, like a mantra—I won't let you be just aloe and *putush*. I'll turn you into paddy. Dhatua? I'll turn you into paddy.

When the seedlings appear, everyone comes to see them. Lachman, Makhan or Ramlagan's fertilizer-fed seedlings are nothing in comparison. These seedlings are as green as they are healthy.

—Fallow land, new seedlings. Everyone says so. Dulan, irritated, drives everyone away. He'll do the ploughing and sowing himself, and savour the fresh green by himself.

The *pahaan* says—Lachman Singh would have died of envy if he'd seen this.

—Who? Dulan is indifferent.

—Lachman Singh.

—Where is he?

—Gone to Gaya. To his in-laws' place.

—Oh!

Then the paddy grows. Tall, strong, healthy plants. A wonderful crop. The paddy ripens. Now Dulan's extreme insanity is revealed.

He says—I'm not going to harvest the crop.

—What? After all the labour of cutting a canal and draining out the stagnant water this past monsoon, after staying there day and night, after I wore myself to death carting your *ghato* and water from home each day—you won't reap?

—No. And no one is to come there. I've work to do.

—What work? Just sitting?

—Yes. Just sitting.

What he was waiting for occurred. Lachman returned for the harvest. The news of Dulan's bumper crop came to his ears. A year has passed since Dhatua's murder. Lachman is in control of himself again.

Lachman came to Dulan. Dulan knew he would come. He knew.

—Dulan.

—*Malik*, protector?

—Come here.

—What's this, you're alone?

—Don't talk rubbish. What's the meaning of this?

—What?

—Why is there paddy on this land?

—I farmed it.

—What was agreed between us?

—You tell me.

—Son of a bitch, didn't I tell you not to farm this land? To leave it as jungle—

Dulan below, Lachman on horseback. All at once, Dulan grabbed Lachman's foot and pulled hard. Lachman fell. His gun was hurled away. The gun in

Dulan's hand. Before Lachman could gather his wits, the *butt* of the gun slammed into his head. Lachman screamed. Dulan smashed the *butt* into his *collar bone.* A snapping sound.

—Son of a bitch, bastard . . . Frightened, Lachman realized that he was crying before Dulan. Tears of agony and terror. He, Lachman Singh, prostrate on the ground, and Dulan Ganju standing erect? He lunged at Dulan's foot and winced in pain. Dulan had thrown a rock at his hand. It would be a long time before he could use his right hand again.

—Animal! Cur!

—What was our agreement, *malik?* That I shouldn't farm. Why not? You'll sow corpses, and I'll guard them. Why? Otherwise you'll burn down the village, kill my family. Very good. But, *malik,* seven boys—seven. Is it right for only wild, thorny underbrush to grace their graves? So, I sowed paddy, you see. Everyone says I've gone mad. I have, you know. I won't let you go today, *malik,* I won't let you harvest your crop. Won't let you shoot, burn houses, kill people. You've harvested enough.

—Do you think the police will let you go?

—If they don't, they don't. Your henchmen, too, will probably go for me. But when haven't they, *malik?* Has the police ever let up on us? So they'll beat me—if I die, so be it. Everyone dies sometime. Did Dhatua die before his death?

Now, knowing that he is totally helpless, Lachman Singh is filled with the fear of death. But even in the throes of this fear, in southeast Bihar the Rajput will never beg the lowborn for mercy. Even if he did, the lowborn will not always be able to gift him his life. As

Dulan could not.

As Lachman tried his best to stand up, shout, or lift a stone with his left hand, Dulan said—What a pity *malik*! You had to die by a Ganju's hand!

He began to smash in Lachman's head with a rock. Over and over again. Lachman is a professional killer, he knows the value of a bullet, murder does not upset him. He would have killed Dulan with a single bullet.

Dulan is not used to killing, a rock has no value, this death is the result of years of intense mental turmoil. He continued to smash Lachman's head in.

Then it was no longer necessary. Dulan stood up. There are many things to be done, one by one. He led the horse forward by the reins, brought a stick down on its haunches and drove it off. Let it go where it will. He lashed Lachman, gun and all, with a rope, and dragged him away. Dumped him in a ditch. Then he rolled stone after stone into it. Stone after stone. Laughter begins to well up inside him. So, *malik* protector, you're like the disgusting Oraon-Munda? Buried under stones? A stony grave?

No telltale signs are likely to remain on the hard rocky ground. But he broke a leafy branch off a nearby *putush* bush to sweep away marks of the struggle. Then he climbed onto the *machaan*.

The search for Lachman continued for a few days. Since he never consulted anyone, Lachman had not mentioned that he was going to see Dulan. This was only natural, since his dependence on Dulan had to be kept secret. Those of his henchmen who knew kept their mouths shut. When the *malik* protector himself is missing, when his horse is discovered grazing on Daitari Singh's land, why irritate a fresh wound? Lachman's servant said—He drank his sweetened milk as usual, and rode off. How do I know where he went?

A very strange business. Only when the hyenas began to howl did people smell a rat. That too, five days later. For five days, the scavengers, smelling flesh beneath the stones, howled, and with great effort shifted the stones, but managed to devour only the face. The strategic cunning with which the corpse was concealed, plus the presence of the horse in his fields, led to Daitari being suspected. Lachman's son supported this view and, because of an old history of feuds, Daitari was questioned for a few days. Then the police give up for lack of evidence, though Lachman's son and Daitari continue the old tradition of conflict. At no stage do suspicions centre on Dulan. It is natural not to suspect him. It is impossible to imagine Dulan killing Lachman, whatever the circumstances.

On the one hand, Lachman-related investigations continue, on the other, a new, contented Dulan descends from the *machaan*. He speaks to the *pahaan*, and as a result all of Kuruda village gathers in the *pahaan's* courtyard one evening. Dulan says—I've never given anyone anything, ever.

Everyone is stunned.

—All of you praised my crop. When I didn't harvest it, you said I was mad. While I was farming, you called me mad. You called this fool a fool. Now listen to what this madman has to say.

—Go ahead!

There is a sense of relief after Lachman's death. Right now, no one wants to worry about the son taking on the father's role.

—My paddy is your seed. Take it.

—You're giving it away?

—Yes, take it, reap it. There's a long story behind this—

—Did you use fertilizer?

—Yes I did, very precious fertilizer. Dulan's voice disappears like the string of a severed kite losing itself in the sky. Then, clearing his throat he says—You harvest it. Give me some, as well. I'll sow it again and again.

After they promise that they will harvest the crop when the time comes, Dulan returns to his land. His heart is strangely, wonderfully light today! He stands on the embankment and looks at the paddy.

Karan, Asrafi, Mohar, Bulaki, Mahuban, Paras and Dhatua—what an amazing joy there is in the ripe green paddy nourished on your flesh and bones! Because you will be seed. To be a seed is to stay alive. Slowly, Dulan climbs up to the *machaan*. A tune in his heart. Stubbornly disobedient. Returning time and again. Dhatua made up this song. Dhatua—Dulan's voice trembles as he says the name. Dhatua, I've turned you all into seed.

the witch

Adivasi' / low caste

N<small>O RAIN</small> in the month of *Chaitra.* A
fiery *Baisakh* and *Jaisthya* come and
go, and the monsoon month of *Ashad* is as fierce as
Dhumavati. Clouds play hide and seek. Kuruda's
philosophical pessimist Budhni Oraon says with grave
satisfaction—Oh, this time we'll have drought for sure,
and famine as well, I just know it.

They were filling water from the softly trickling
Kuruda river. Sanichari said—Yes, the signs are very
ominous. Have you seen the vultures and kites circling
in the sky?

Moti says—This time the *sarkar* won't let us starve.
They'll start distributing *khhichri* in time.

Budhni says—Have you heard?

A man's come. There's *relief* at Tohri. Road
construction work. They'll give daily wages, *khhichri*,
milo.

anthropomorphism?

Budhni says—Why should we wait for the famine? Let's go beforehand. Let the famine come and stay by itself in the deserted village.

No one paid much attention to these words at the time, but soon enough they take on a new meaning, and everyone says that the words 'Let the famine come and stay in the deserted village', were an inauspicious invitation. Kuruda is now inviting wickedness and misfortune. A vulture is supposed to have snatched the words from the air and conveyed them to the *daini*.

The *daini* was searching for a home at the time. Everything that happened along with the famine is due to the *daini*.

It seems that children are drinking the *soyabean* relief milk, vomiting, falling over, and dying. Cattle are dying. Ravens are tilting off branches and whirling down, dead. All because of the *daini*.

There's nothing fixed about this *daini* business. Men or women whom you meet every day may suddenly become *dains* or *dainis*. If there is a *daini* in the vicinity, astonishing things happen, which no one has ever seen, though everyone has heard about them.

It seems that in Murhai, when an old Ganju woman struck a flint to light her *beedi*, the stones yielded blood instead of sparks. It seems that somewhere a newborn infant walks down the road kicking a fire-bearing pot before him. It seems that somewhere the Munda dead have shoved aside their gravestones to emerge into the burial ground, where they sit and sing.

No one could figure out why these things were happening. Tura is a Munda village. The *pahaan* there said his young daughter vanished into thin air as she was returning to Tura from Tahar.

Total chaos. Terror everywhere. Finally, everyone approached Hanuman Misra of Tahar. A Hindu Brahmin, priest of the Shiva Mandir, and an influential person of the area, Hanumanji fasted and prostrated himself before the gods. Then he said that the gods had sent him an awesome dream. A terrifying, naked woman uttered the words, 'I am famine', before floating away on a bloodsoaked cloud. According to the *panjika*, she is a *daini*. This *daini* has to be found and driven away. If she is wounded, if she bleeds, or if she is burnt to death, a terrible calamity will be visited upon them.

The *daini* is supposed to be moving about with Kuruda, Murhai, Hesadi and other such villages as her base.

Because these and all villages like them are dens of sinners.

Hanuman Misra explains the matter of sin thus— They are great sinners. Or else, during the Naxal upheaval, JP movement, Emergency, why would the police ransack their villages? How come they did not touch the higher castes? They are big sinners, these Ganju–Dushad–Dhobi–Oraon–Mundas. The last two groups are the worst. Today they worship their own barbaric gods, tomorrow Jesus in the *missions*, the day after, the Hindu gods! They show no discretion in the matter of worship. So they get no protection or patronage from any particular god during famine–drought–police attacks.

—They must be major sinners. Or else, why would they die in famines or floods? They aren't ashamed of begging. They're bone idle, yet say they can't get work.

The *daini* finds a conducive atmosphere in such sinful places. And yet, if they cannot find and chase away the *daini,* they will perish.

Having said this much, Hanuman Misra unleashed a nameless horror of the unknown into the atmosphere. People began to wilt in unnamed terror.

Everyone began to suspect everyone else, to mistrust the behaviour of near and dear ones.

Sodan Ganju of Murhai noticed his old mother going out at night and followed her. His mother squatted in the courtyard, did her business as usual, and rose. When he came back in and closed the door, it suddenly seemed to Sodan that the person lying on the straw mat was not his mother. Demented with terror, Sodan ran out, yelling, and summoned his neighbours. They fetched lamps and made Sodan's mother walk, to check if her feet touched the ground, or whether she cast a shadow. Then, with a razor they split open the skin of her hand in front of everyone, to check whether her blood was red or black. Only then was the old woman released. Sadness that her own son had thought her a *daini* drove her to visit the shrine of Haramdeo.

She had resolved to starve to death, but as soon as hunger weighted her eyelids, she felt that Sodan was being abducted by the *daini.* Immediately she rose, began to scream—Don't go with her, Sodan! It's the *daini!*—and started to run. Reaching home, she saw that it was just as she had expected! Sodan was chasing a female porcupine. She threw a stone that struck Sodan's leg; only by laming her son could she save him from the *daini.* The *daini* in the form of the porcupine, her plot foiled, fled.

All husbands–fathers–brothers–sons were compelled to keep watch upon the women. Do they cast shadows on the ground; when they return from the fields after defecating or urinating, does a crow fly above their heads; is the person who finishes the outdoor-work at night and returns to latch the door the same as the person who went out—a strict surveillance was maintained to note all this. It's not easy to hunt a *daini*. Everyone, everywhere, has to suspect everyone else, all the time. Hence, a few mishaps are bound to occur, and they do.

Every year, during times of famine, Hesadi's Daitar Dushad hands his mother a tin bowl and seats her at the *bus junction*. He did the same this year. Every year, Daitar's mother begs for a month or two, and sleeps beneath the banyan tree. Near the bus *cleaners*. The *cleaners* also sleep beneath the banyan, in the stifling heat. Beyond the shade of the tree, on a cemented platform. Every year, they hear Daitar's mother babbling in her sleep. This year, they rebelled after the very first night. They said, which ghoul was she calling at night? To whom was she saying, Come, come?

Daitar's old mother did not completely comprehend the seriousness of the situation. She smiled toothlessly and said—The black cow! I dreamt that the wretch was refusing to enter the cow shed. As a result, the *case* against her attains serious proportions—Dreams, a black cow, the inauspicious colour black, and that, too, calling out to it! The *cleaners* said—Scram! Or we'll stone you.

Most suprisingly, while the old woman was trudging the three miles back home, she toppled over head-first, hit the ground and died. Thanks to the greedy, impatient jackals, Daitar didn't even have to perform her last rites. Within a short while, everyone was certain that not jackals but the *daini* herself had devoured

Daitar's mother.

The human nervous system revolts against the unremitting tension of fear. If the terror of famine is added to this, the sinners are unable to bear the double burden.

Those who provide *relief*, like the *relief officer*, *mission* workers, the *sadhus* of the *seva sangh*, all noticed the suppressed violence and hardness in the eyes and faces of the downtrodden. Eyes as restless as the tide, searching for something. Very surprising. Because in their experience the adivasis of these areas are by nature totally unfeeling. During a famine, they abandon their children at the *mission* gates and disappear. If their village is burnt down, they don't return to it in a hurry. If explanations are sought, they say—The children will die if they stay with us; at least in the *mission* they'll stay alive. We don't return if our houses are burnt down because we build houses of mud and leaves. An iron pot and the *baloa* at our waist are the only things in our houses that are bought with cash. What should we go back for?

In times of famine they have seen the extreme indifference of these people. An impenetrable wall is raised before their faces, their eyes—it is impossible to cross this barrier and evoke some human interest. Social service women have tried waving rattles in the faces of skeletal children in the arms of skeletal mothers who have come for *relief*, cooing encouragingly—Look, baby, look, a toy! The children stare out with unfeeling indifference from the other side of a glass wall.

This time, their faces are full of life. Harsh, restless, alert.

More *reports* add to the unease. From the village-service groups.

For example—Earlier, if pariah dogs entered the village, the local mongrels would chase them away.

Now, human beings stone them with heartless cruelty and drive them out.

After collecting *relief*, everyone sleeps around a blazing fire, even in this heat. Men take turns to keep watch.

Relief is as firmly bound up with *injections* and vaccinations as the seven-time-repeated matrimonial vows. Every year, a lady doctor or *missionary* or even a female medical student would administer *injections* and vaccinations to uncomplaining patients. This time, they refuse to take the needle from a female outsider.

A wealthy middle-aged lady desirous of offering *relief* was on her way to Tohri, her *station wagon* fitted with a loudspeaker blaring 'Krishna Consciousness' hymns. On the way, she entered a village to ask for water. Neither she nor the other white *sannyasinis* got any. They were pelted with stones. This broke their hearts and they said—If Krishna in his famine form has been unable to awaken humane feelings in these people, then what Lord Krishna desires for them is death by starvation. They did not go to Tohri. Taking all the *relief* materials with them—money, rice, milk-powder and medicines— they returned to Patna.

These events have made the village-service workers very anxious. They realize that, in anticipation of some calamity, a current of terror is flowing from village to village. They know that something is changing in the mental make-up of these people.

How can this be remedied? They hear that in order to replace the bestiality in their hearts with spiritual feelings, Hanuman Misra is desirous of feeding a sacrificial fire with one *quintal* of *ghee* over seven days; and that the white *secretary* of the 'Krishna Consciousness' *ashram* in Patna has offered to provide the required *ghee*. On one condition. As the *ghee* is poured in, the praise of Shiva, *Shivastotram,* is to be recited in a low key. Because, at the same time, these people will be playing 'Lord Krishna, where are you?' in their *station wagon* parked outside. This has put Hanuman Misra in a quandary. He has no quarrel with Krishna *sangeet.* After all, He who is *Har* is also *Hari*— both Shiva and Krishna. He is worried about the *ghee.* It is cow's-milk *ghee,* all right, but made from the milk of *Australian* cows. Shiva is a hot-tempered god. Suppose he throws a tantrum because *Australia* is beyond his ken? The Hindu gods are masters of the world. But when they were so designated, *Australia* hadn't yet been discovered. So, Misra is unable to consent.

The abovementioned white gentleman has heard about the *daini,* and requested Misraji not to kill her. If he can find a genuine *Bharatiya daini,* he'll take her to his own land. He has also decreed that if the *daini* is to be found, it is essential for everyone to mistrust everyone else, wholesale. He has said—if need be, mistrust yourself as well.

Misraji has taken this to heart. He has said—Oh, wretched ones! Alone you wander the fields, the hills, the forests. It's your duty to check if you're casting a shadow, or if a crow, kite or vulture is circling above your head.

Suspect yourself, spy on yourself, these directives lead to all kinds of tumult and confusion in the hearts of these terrorized people. The *daini* has to be found, but not killed.

The Kůruda *pahaan* says—I don't understand. There's never been a *dain* like this before. That time, when Sanichari's father's sister was named a *daini*—

He stops abruptly. And in his eyes, in the eyes of the listeners, a spark of cunning flashes. They had murdered the old woman by stoning her to death, and because the hyenas had made a dinner of her, the police could not arrest them.

He says—What's up this time? Has everyone changed?

Sanichari's son says—I don't know, Misraji of Tahar has put such fear into our hearts!

Everything is strange! They came, brought *relief,* went away again. Look, shreds of clouds straggle about in the sky. The paddy seedlings are limp. The leaves are as dry as a pregnant woman's tongue. The other day, Bisra Ganju's wife gave birth to a son. The baby had a tooth in his mouth. Wolf–hyena–jackal roam the village paths in broad daylight.

Perhaps Sengel-da will come again. The sky will rain fire. Everything will burn. Are the gods as powerful as they once were? Can they fashion a new earth once again?

This discussion occurs in the morning. At night, the *pahaan's* wife hears the *pahaan* crying out—Come, come, come to me. Come to me.

—Who're you calling?

—My shadow. I went out to piss, my shadow went with me. I've come back inside, no shadow.

—No shadow?

—No.

—How come?

—It seems I've turned into a *dain!*

This makes it clear that even the *pahaan*, the chief priest, who is in direct communication with the gods, is not immune to the grip of terror. The *pahaan's* wife is more strongminded than her husband. She lit two *dibris* and then said to her husband—There's your shadow. Can a *dain* ever get the *pahaan?*

It was evident that the *pahaan's* mental geography was cracked and fissured, his self-confidence shaken. Why else would he think himself a *dain* in the middle of the night?

After this, Budhni Oraon, gathering wood in the Kuruda forest, saw the reflection of a hairy arm in a pond. In a flash it came to her—she was turning into a *daini*. She threw away the wood and crawled to the edge of the pond, to watch her own transformation with total concentration. Catching sight of another hairy arm, she shrieked 'I'm a *daini!*' so loudly that even an animal as dangerous as the bear was startled and, leaping over her crouched form, took to its heels. Only then did Budhni return to her senses, and, flinging away the wood, she fled towards the village.

One day Bisra Dushad of Burudiha killed his only material asset, a young black cow. A cow is just a cow. But when Bisra drinks *moua*, the cow turns into a young woman and beckons to him. The death of a black cow can ruin the life of someone like Bisra Dushad, and it does. For a few days, Bisra sat in a stupor, like a madman with bloodshot eyes, in the empty cowshed. Then he realized that without the cow he was doomed. The cow could no longer grow to maturity, birth calves, yield milk and help pay back the debt incurred in buying it,

which meant more debt for survival. At the thought of
this, he took the tethering-rope and hanged himself
from the rafters of his cowshed. At night. That same
evening he had bought his son a top. Mended the
thatch on his hut. Told his wife—See, the cow wasn't a
daini, after all. I killed the poor, helpless thing for
nothing.

His wife had thought her husband was coming back
to normal after a temporary lapse of reason.

Bisra Dushad was the best *gunin* in the area; he
knew the medicinal qualities of all the herbs and plants.
The only hope when the villagers fell sick. He was also a
water-diviner. He knew where water could be found
under the earth. Such a man's death is a direct attack
on the structure of village society. He was necessary to
this village seeped in age-old darkness. It may not have
led to a debt-free, easy life, but it did earn him respect.
Poverty and destitution, to the Birsa Dushads of this
world, are as inevitable and all-pervasive as the air and
the sky. Bisra had no particular grouse against the lack
of an easy life. Neither he nor the others had such a life.
In the *communism* of poverty, the Dushad–Ganju–
Oraon–Munda belong to the same class, they're
'comrades'.

—Fear of the *daini* caused Bisra's death,' the *pahaan*
proclaimed. Today Bisra has gone, suppose tomorrow
Bhurai Lohar, the ironsmith, dies? How will we get our
work done? What if the following day Bharat dies, who
will do our carpentry jobs? Hunt out the *daini*. I'll
prostrate myself before the gods, I'll go on a fast, you
need not fear, no harm will come to you.

News of the *daini*-terror gradually came to the ears
of the village-service organization, and they informed

the local official of the Adivasi Welfare Ministry. In his capacity as a government official, he informed the police. Because if old men and women are murdered in a *daini*-hunt, it becomes a punishable offence. His responsibility ended there. Then, forgetting his identity as an official bureaucrat, he became an individual once again, and, trembling with fear, rushed to Hanuman Misra, and paid him fifty-one rupees for a sacred charm to ward off evil.

The *thana daroga* says—There hasn't yet been a murder in the name of *daini*-hunting. And even if there is, what can I do? I'm a government servant. If a harijan is killed, I'll *report* the death. But if the killer is not a Brahmin or Rajput, if an adivasi or scheduled caste kills one of his brethren? As a *daini*? Then I'll go on leave. I won't interfere in the matter of *dainis*. *Sarkars* come and go. But *dainis* are forever. Who wants to die of a *daini's* curse?

And in this way, events circle blindly in a labyrinth. The unfathomable terror of the *daini* is like a maze. You can enter, but you can't find your way out. Then, one day, there is a commotion in Murhai village. Burning brands dance against the sky, a grotesque scream rends the air—*Aah–anh–anh!* The *daini* has been found.

There is an age-old connection between the word '*daini*' and Murhai village. As usual, the villagers are Ganjus and Dushads. Those who think that in these parts caste problems occur only between upper and lower castes, don't fully understand the issue.

Like the famous line from *The Arabian Nights*—*puriya ke andar puriya, uske andar puriya*—in the matter of caste and community, too, there are stories within stories. Dig for an earthworm and, unwittingly, you'll unearth a *dinosaur.*

That Hanuman Misra will not allow Bhola Ganju near his well is an attitude Bhola both understands and accepts the fairness of.

But on the other hand, Bharat Dushad is higher in the caste hierarchy than Bhola Ganju, and Bhola and Bharat are both higher than Ramrik Dhobi, the washerman. A variety of problems. Problems which appear ridiculous to the Oraon and Munda people. They don't follow this caste system. And because they don't, Bharat, Bhola, and Ramrik all think they're stupid.

Almost every village has an Oraon or Munda *bustee.* Interestingly, the Oraon or Munda *pahaan* or chief priest's authority is unquestioningly accepted even by the non-adivasi Ganjus, Dushads and Dhobis.

Murhai village suffers from endemic hunger–starvation–famine–drought–bonded labour–*mahajan* oppression etc. When these misfortunes plague them a little less, they immediately fall to squabbling over caste differences, which they settle to keep life eventful.

Each area has its own special characteristics. The women of Hesadi are bad-tempered; the Oraons of Kuruda lazy, the men of Burudi quarrelsome. And every ten-fifteen years, some old man or woman of Murhai becomes a *daini.*

Then they shoot arrows at others' cattle, lure someone's wife out into the night and bite her after turning into puppies, or change into rats and chew up sacks of corn and paddy.

Once, after Shivratri, the children began to vomit milk, stiffen and die, one after the other. The government doctor said—They bathed the Shiva idol in

Misraji's temple with milk and collected all that milk in a vat—if you feed that stale milk to the children, how d'you expect them not to die?

No one contradicted him. Ramrik's wife buried her three-year-old daughter and gathered together her caste brethren. They hold a discussion in the dark. Then they go to Mahuri Dhobin's house. Mahuri is old, her skin hangs in folds, she has a huge appetite. It was she who had fetched the milk that killed Ramrik's daughter.

They set fire to the thatch of Mahuri's hut and drag her out. Half-burnt, hounded out, in fear and agony, she stumbles on the stones, falls flat on her face and dies.

This was an attack with intent to kill. Ramrik and his cousin, his younger uncle's son, are still in jail.

About ten years before this, Roto Munda's widow had become a *daini*. Fortunately, as soon as they cut off her nose and let the blood flow, she became human again. It was not necessary to kill her.

The reason for these accounts is to show that *daini*s are fond of Murhai. In this wretched place, god knows why, when the wind sighs through the *kash* groves, it sounds like a lament, *hai, hai, hai.*

Murhai is where the *daini* is first caught. The cause—the taboo inter-caste love between the abovementioned Ramrik Dhobi's son and Baram Ganju's widowed sister.

A wretched love in a wretched place. Here, due to stringent caste laws, such illegitimate love can never lead to fulfilment. Even so, love appears sometimes, and those whom it attacks are bruised black and blue.

Ramrik's son Parsad and Baram's sister Mani have known each other since childhood. Parsad's wife is a friend of Mani's. Mani's husband, too, was an acquaintance of Parsad's. By village norms, Mani is Parsad's son's *pishi*. Suddenly, while dancing at the Karam festival, they fell in love.

In a few days, their eyes began to search each other out. In a few days, they began to plan ways to meet each other on the way home from the market or from the jungle, dragging firewood. Finally, they were discovered.

Parsad's wife came and abused Mani, went home and sat down to cry.

Baram announced his pious intention of hacking his sister to death and went off to get *kerosene* on his *permit*.

Ramrik's mother is intelligent and farsighted. She came to Baram's house and, sitting carefully in the courtyard so that nothing was defiled by her touch, she pulled at the hookah for a while. Then she said—What's done is done. No point making a noise about it. My daughter-in-law is a shrivelled-up hag. My virile son isn't satisfied. Mani is a barren widow. Hot blood coursing through the veins can arouse even a castrated goat. You handle your own household.

The village elders called Baram and Ramrik together and said—For the past few years, the police have been harassing us for no reason. Then there was drought, followed by famine. And now there's this threat of the *daini*. Is this any time to begin an illicit affair? How can we be sure that the *daini* is not behind this? Let's not make trouble over this. Each of you, sort out your own household. If things get out of hand, we'll give them both a sound thrashing.

If you think about it, these words are really pathetic and heart-wrenching. And significant as well. Till a few years ago, the *mahajan's* oppression, starvation, famine

and drought had not destroyed their mental strength.
All this is part of their life, anyway.

Once upon a time, the Kuruda river did not exist; it
was formed two hundred years ago when the Koel
changed its course—but to these people, the river must
have been there forever, because it's been there since
their fathers' and grandfathers' time.

Similarly, they cannot imagine a time when there
was no *mahajan-jotedar* in their lives. Their fathers and
grandfathers have lived under the tyranny of the
mahajan-jotedar. Hence, this cursed oppression must
have been there forever, as well.

But police oppression has not always existed. The
Naxal upheaval—the JP movement— the Emergency—
they could not understand why the police was harassing
them. But their lives are under attack.

Despite the *mahajan's* tyranny, famine and drought,
the village society was still keen on punishing
infringements of caste rules. But the police oppression
has sucked the sap from their lives.

Now, neither the will nor the desire to punish Mani
and Parsad remain. Every able-bodied man and woman
is indispensable to the village economy. It's not feasible
to drive these two out.

Hamru, the village elder, cleared his throat and
said—Parsad! Mani! We're as good as dead. Don't add
to our suffering. If we drive you out, where'll you go?
What'll you do? What will happen to Parsad's wife and
children?

Parsad and Mani had expected to be thrashed with
shoes, driven out or flogged. Everything was topsy-turvy.
Instantly filled with remorse, they prostrated themselves
and vowed to think of each other only as brother and

sister.

But love is a difficult disease to cure. For a few days Mani was very quiet. Baram told her—After the harvest season, I'll get you married again. Your younger brother-in-law has grown up now, and he's interested.

This brought tears to Mani's eyes. She felt her older brother's sympathy. And from the wrenching pain his words brought, she realized how much she loved Parsad. Softly she said—We'll see about that. Let's get the harvesting done first.

—Harvest! With no sign of rain!

—It'll rain.

—How can it? When the clouds just wander here and there, not standing still for a moment.

In their shared anxiety about the poor *bhutta* and *maroa* crop due to the lack of rain, brother and sister feel close to each other for an instant. When his father died, Baram was plunged into a sea of troubles, aggravated by a lazy wife and an aged mother. When Mani came back, brother and sister managed to bring some order into the household. Mani was solely responsible for harvesting, winnowing, threshing and taking the crop to market. Baram said—Forget about Parsad.

—I will.

—It's not right to break up a neighbour's home.

—Yes.

Mani accepted every word. Then she said—You'd better re-thatch the house. Water seeps in.

—Do you have ropes?

—Yes. And you can get two lengths from Bhura. He borrowed them from us.

—I will.

Talk of thatch reminded them that Parsad was very good at making sturdy rope from the fibre of the aloe tree, with which he would bind thatch so well that it lasted for years. Heaving a deep sigh, Mani took her scythe and went off to the forest.

Parsad had marked this. Two or three days later, he joined Mani in the forest. Mani and Parsad knew that it was wrong to meet like this. This love could not bring them happiness. Yet they fell into each other's arms.

The jungle. A bed of leaves. Coming together in immense despair, knowing that they couldn't hold on to this. Mani returning with tearful eyes.

They had both seen it.

On a stone in the heart of the almost black Kuruda river, sat a dark, near-naked, terrifying young woman, her stomach distended, gnawing the raw flesh of a bird. A *tatui* bird, which lives near water. It's flesh is fatty. Catching sight of them, the woman glares out of terrible, cruel eyes, snarls, and then, swaying from side to side, begins to scream—*anh-anh-anh*! Like an ox. An ox being branded with a red-hot iron. *Mahajan* Golbadan has a thousand oxen which have to be branded thus. Or else, they are stolen and sold in the Tahar cattle market.

—*Daini*! Parsad and Mani gasped in fear. Then, forgetting to hide that they had met secretly, they ran to the village. The villagers of Murhai had not abandoned their village in the famine. Kuruda and Hesadi were deserted. Everyone had sought shelter in Tohri.

Hearing the news, the village elder, sensing danger, sounds the *nagara* drum. The deep, gruff voice of the *nagara* signals the approach of danger. Everyone knows from the quickening of the blood that this *nagara* is being sounded because of the *daini*. There is no water in Kuruda river, so it can't be a flood. No fire has broken out, no wild elephant has attacked the crop. This must be the *daini*.

   —*Daini?*
   —*Daini.*
   —Where?
   —In the heart of Kuruda.
   —Doing what?
   —Eating the raw flesh of a bird.
   —Then?
   —We have to drive her out.
   —Why?
   —What else do we do?
   —Kill her.
   —No-o!

The *pahaan* shrieked. He was not bound to follow Hanuman Misra's orders, because he was not a Hindu. But he knows that he has no option. Hanuman Misra's power and influence are all-encompassing, he is wealthy, he has the police and government officials, the *mahajans* and *jotedars,* under his thumb, so when he gives orders to the contrary, one must automatically forget one's ancient right to burn a *daini* to death.

Trembling with fear, the *pahaan* struck the *nagara* with a shrivelled hand. Told the villagers—Everything is different these days! I've never seen a drought like this, a sky like this. Even the *daini* is different!

   —Different!
   —Yes.

Alert as a wary animal, the *pahaan* turned his wrinkled neck. The *daini* sucks blood with her eyes, devours the life of little children.

—Of course!

—This *daini* breathes death. Her breath drives the clouds away, makes trees barren, withers the *maroa* field crop, this is a different sort of *daini*.

Parsad and Baram forgot their differences and looked at each other.

—Everyone has the right to kill us, why can't we kill the *daini*?

—Parsad! Will you listen to me or are you doing the talking?

—I don't know! I'm Parsad, and you're the *pahaan*. You tell us, we'll obey. But—

—What?

Parsad clears his throat and says—The Tahar *thakur* told us of our sins, we heard him out. What choice did we have! So we sinned, he called us sinners.

—Why did you say 'but'?

—But . . . are we the only sinners?

—Who's sinned, then? I?

All this while Sanichari had been picking nits from her hair. She said—You don't understand, *pahaan*. You're indispensable during rituals and ceremonies! You talk directly to the gods! If there's been some slip-up in the worship rituals, you're the sinner. If there's no slip-up, there's no sin. Now, are you all going to worry about your own sins, or are we going to chase away the *daini*?

The *pahaan* realizes that he must now take the lead or people will begin to doubt his omnipotence.

He says—The men are to come with me. The women are to go home. Take the children and bar the doors. Parsad, go with the advance party.

—Why? Mani has thrown shame to the winds.

—He's seen her. He'll show us the way.

Dim twilight. The *pahaan* lights a fire, folds his hands and chants the mantra. Everyone, young, aging and old, lights his torch at this fire. Stones tucked into the folds at their waists. Then the *pahaan*, clutching his arms, whirling around, leaps and snatches a torch, circles the fire, smears his chest and forehead with earth, raises his hands to the sky and calls out—*Ha Aaba* Haramdeo, help me to chase away the *daini*!

Saying this, he pricks up his ears and inclines his head. Perhaps his ancient, ineffectual god, exiled to some dark world of the mind, hears his voice and answers. An owl restores the *pahaan's* honour. Terrorized by his hideous cries, the owl shrieks and takes off from the hollow of the *neem* tree much before its usual time. Owls do not generally take flight when afternoon marries evening.

The *pahaan* is very pleased by this, and raising his head, he says—*Deota* has heard us!

Now they begin to run in traditional battle formation. Uttering war cries. From the village to the forest. Down the narrow path, to the heart of the river. On the way, the *pahaan* warns them—Watch out! Be careful with the torches! If the forest catches fire, everyone will be fined, imprisoned. Don't set the forest on fire.

Parsad longs to burn down the forest, challenge the police and Forest Department; he feels reckless. Chasing off the *daini* has made him daring. Suddenly he thinks—normally, he can't run like this. But now he can. Since he can, he should run away with Mani while the impulse still throbs in his veins. Without desperate courage, it is impossible to break the barriers of caste.

Such courage doesn't always fire the blood, as it is doing now. He says—Look there!

They all raise their torches and stop dead. Flickering red flames on Kuruda's dark waters. The black water rushes, foaming, hitting the stones. To the frightened villagers, the rippling water is like the uncoiling of a serpent.

A large rock. On it stands a naked, very dark young woman. Her body is twisted, half visible. Her mouth is covered with feathers and blood. Sighting them, she raises her hand. She is clutching the ripped-off wing of a bird.

—*Daini!*

They all shout together.

The *daini's* eyes gleam in anticipation. She sways from side to side, laughing soundlessly.

—She's laughing!

Shrivelled, wrinkled, skeletal, the *pahaan* moves forward. Fear makes him ferocious. Fear attacks the others too, turning them all violent.

The *pahaan* says—In the name of Haramdeo, in the name of all the *bonga*—we will drive you out.

The *daini*, too, turns aggressive. She raises her hands, shakes her matted hair out of her face, and starts to scream, rending the forest–river–sky with her *anh–anh–anh!* She advances, stepping from stone to stone, with flaming eyes.

—Stone her!

A shower of stones flies through the air. The *daini* also lifts a rock. A stone hits her. Don't let her bleed! Her blood will breed a hundred *dainis!* The *daini's* mouth is a gaping cave.

—Shall we stone her?

—Yes! Stone her!

The *daini* hurls a stone with great force. The *pahaan* is hit on the head. Blood streams down his face.

—Hit her, hit her, or she'll hit us!

Stones fly back and forth. Parsad hurls his torch into the air and leaps up. Flaming torches against the sky. Shriek after ear-splitting shriek. A shower of stones in the dark.

—*Anh–anh–anh*! Screams tear the sky to shreds. The *daini* plunges into the water and, quick as lightning, climbs the opposite bank.

From this bank they pursue her, fling stones, shout.

—*Anh–anh–anh*! Her screams help track her as she flees. Chasing her, the *pahaan* says—She's going towards Hesadi. Let her go. As long as she leaves us alone.

Wiping the blood from his forehead, jubilant with victory, he says—We'll spend the night at the shrine. No sleep tonight. Tonight we'll dance and drink *moua*!

—And tomorrow?

—Why, tomorrow there'll be a *puja*.

Calling on Haramdeo, the *pahaan* runs on. The *daini's* screams gradually fade into the darkness towards the east. They die out.

—She's gone to the Jilad fields!

—Let her go! At this time, the Jilad fields are thick with ghosts and ghouls. She's bound to go there.

At the outskirts of the village they stop dead on the banks of the river, ears to the wind, listening for the *daini's* faint screams. Her voice is swallowed up by the darkness. They wait. Then, silence, like a flood, engulfs them. They drown in it, go under.

Once again they are overcome with the helplessness of drowning men. Their obsession with chasing the *daini* had, for a time, turned these starving, hopeless people—ignored by government and administration alike—into ravaging wolves.

The ebbing of the violence leaves them empty. Suddenly, they get scared. Eye each other.

The *pahaan's* in-built *radar* picks up their change of heart even in the dark. Their minds are soft as river mud. They have to be hardened into *granite* and unleashed in pursuit of the *daini*. But when the *daini* leaves, they turn slack and soggy again.

The *pahaan's* heart swells with tenderness. A fatherly affection for his wretched paupers overpowers him. He forgets that he-is also a starving pauper. In his mind, he is a king.

With great compassion he asks—Why are you so scared? Eh? I can't see your faces in the dark, but there's fear in your voices and breathing.

—Has the *daini* gone?

—Yes, yes, she's gone. The bleeding has stopped. I'm in no pain.

—The *daini's* gone!!

—Yes. Can't you tell? Can't you read the wind?

They turn towards the village. As they walk, each one feels a freedom from poison and pain. An auspicious wind. Sanichari's grandson said—Now there'll be fish in the Kuruda river. Oh! She had hidden all the fish.

The *pahaan* spoke in deep faith—There will be rain, the crops will prosper. They can chase away clouds, make crops vanish, if you set a trap in the fields, they hide the rabbits and porcupines.

—Will there be a *puja*?

—Tomorrow.

—And today?

—Singing–dancing–*moua*. Sing your heart out. Baram, fetch your *dholak* from the house.

—Can I tie a sash around my waist and imitate Golbadan?

—*Dhut!* This isn't Holi, you don't have to clown around!

—*Moua?*

—We'll get it from Neemchand. He promised me some, and hasn't given it yet. He'll definitely give it now.

Baram said—Isn't Neemchand's distillery on the way to Hesadi? Why go all that way at night? I'll provide the *moua*.

Fires were lit at the *pahaan's* shrine. The *pahaan* took this step because it wasn't safe to sleep that night. As far as he knew, *dainis* had to be killed. This was the first time he'd heard of them being just chased away. Fear of the unknown is the worst fear, a formless fear. The *daini* might well return. It's best to stay awake all night.

Just the day before, Baram had sneaked out ten bottles of prime *moua* from Neemchand's distillery, aided and abetted by Neemchand's servant. Thirty rupees worth. Selling it in the market would fetch hard cash. Half his, half the servant's. He had used all his cunning to smuggle in the bottles and hide them in straw. Today, in this hour of danger, he brought out this *maal*.

He made the offer partly in order to irritate his kith and kin. If he could share ten bottles of *moua*, they should also offer their secret stashes of toddy. His kinsfolk, in turn, brought out their toddy to shame the others. If they could share their toddy, so could

everyone else. Is there a single household without its
stock of toddy?

Sanichari and the other women turned up with fried
rice, fried corn, onions and chillies. She told the
pahaan—We're too scared to stay at home. We've
brought onions and chillies. Can't we drink *moua*, too?

The *pahaan*'s face lit up with smiles. He said—You
girls are really clever! How can I refuse?! Drink. I'll
contribute your share of the toddy.

Moua and toddy. Spicy fried corn. The throbbing of
the *nagara*. Now Baram began to sing, and the others
took up the chorus. After a long time, the village was
festive again. Under the *moua*'s spell, their hearts felt
light. Ever since Hanuman Misra's pronouncement,
they had been trapped in the coils of *daini*-terror.

When everyone was a little intoxicated and high on
the singing, in fits of laughter as Sanichari wriggled her
ruined hips in dance, Parsad and Mani's eyes met.

There was something about this night, this
atmosphere. Parsad inclined his head. They both slowly
began backing off one step at a time until they stood
behind the *pahaan*'s house.

Parsad took Mani's hand. There was something
about this night, this atmosphere. Mani gave herself up
to Parsad.

They both began to run. Not towards Hesadi,
towards Tohri. In their narrow, restricted lives, Tohri is
the gateway to the world. From Tohri, you can ride a
timber *truck* to Ranchi, Hazaribagh, Dhanbad.

The *pahaan*'s wife saw them go. She said nothing.
Parsad's wife despised her as barren, never accepted
prasad from her. The *pahaani* now got her own back.

The next day, of course, she told the whole village.

How can those who first spied the *daini* be expected to withstand the lure of immorality? Thus, the story of Parsad and Mani's elopement was woven into the *daini* legend and won a wider perspective.

Many people may have read about the Kuruda *belt daini* incident in a racy belles-lettrist essay published in an American magazine, complete with coloured pictures. Of course, not everyone will have been able to read it, since the magazine currently costs twelve rupees, and nowadays buying and reading this particular magazine is considered part of modern education. Those who are busy fighting the English language in the interests of the nation, also read it stealthily on their whirlwind tours from *meeting* to *meeting*, and, by way of an excuse, say, Isn't it imperative to keep abreast of what the opposition is thinking? But in fact those who run this magazine have no idea that these *meeting*-bound babus consider them the 'opposition'. In this way, in this world, essential facts remain hidden, and once again the poet's words prove true—'Long live the unknown!'

These babus are great lovers of archaeology. Getting rid of English, they explain that the English language will soon be relegated to museums.

Since English is bound to be wiped out or expire in *Bharat-bhumi,* they generally educate their own children in English-medium schools. The mental process of these babus is very complex or very simple. This mentality makes them hasten the collective deaths of the *dhokra* metal craftsman or the Purulia mask maker or the terracotta sculptor who crafts horses, while exclaiming 'people's art!' on seeing their work in Calcutta.

How the Kuruda *daini* becomes international news is equally exciting news. The author of the article is none other than the white-skinned Krishna devotee who had offered to supply Hanuman Misra with pure *ghee* from *Australia*. This white man's name is Peter Bharati. He has been in Bharat for years, in different incarnations. In his incarnation of Lokbharati's crazily poetic student, he would wander the *sal* forests, singing the Tagore song 'This is what pleases me.'

In a change of guise, he went back to his native land and, returning about a year later, in the manifestation of a student of History, ensconced himself on the Bharat–Nepal *border*. At that time, History abandoned, he occupied himself with drawing *maps* of the *border*. Once again he disappeared to his native land.

In his new manifestation he came back to Bharat as a mountain-specialist geologist, and, though he knew full well that Calcutta had no mountains, stayed put in the city all through the Decade of Liberation, busying himself with apparently simple things. Simple things like photographing the graffiti on Calcutta's walls, beggars, Kalighat goat sacrifices, and overflowing *dustbins*. He danced with the *sannyasis* in Puddupukur during the Charak festival mela. He joined the *gwalas* on their pilgrimage to Tarakeshwar. Busy doing all this, he suddenly lost consciousness at the Grand Hotel in front of a horde of *reporters* and *photographers*.

When he came to, he was a metamorphosed saheb. Immediately, he revealed that in his dreams, a gigantic *sannyasi* had said to him—Oh crazy one! How long will you search for the touchstone?

So saying, he parted his jaws; and within his open

mouth, Peter saw his Indian incarnations down the ages. And then, inside his open mouth, Peter also saw a picture of Patna Station. Ergo, Patna was his destiny, his ordained destination.

In his final incarnation, Peter arrived in Patna, and, through the mercy of Krishna, everything was fixed in a trice. The *ashram* of Krishna Awareness, national and international *sevak-sevikas*, row upon row of *station wagons*, an endless flow of money. Because many wealthy people with brimming eyes feel themselves blessed as they hand Peter *blank cheques*. Swami Anandabharati initiated Peter into holy orders, transformed him into Peter Bharati, handed over the reins of the *ashram* to him, and took an *aeroplane* to Himachal.

Peter Bharati's Bharat *premkatha*—the legend of his love for Bharat—is well known. From one birth to the next, everything is linked. His *ashram* is for Lokbharati's *sal*-forest-loving ex-students and for the *hippies* of Nepal; all day long the ashram's atmosphere is filled with soothing music piped through hidden *stereos*. As a result, you begin to feel happy as soon as you enter.

After coming into contact with Hanuman Misra, Peter Bharati first hears about the *daini*, and gets interested. Because the Indian pantheon has been endlessly kind to Peter Bharati, he begins to follow the story.

Not on his own. In Tohri, he finds Sharan Mathur. Mathur is a schoolteacher, his father-in-law is Chief Reporter of a Patna-based Hindi daily. Therefore, once in a while Mathur sends off brief reports on local news items; seeing his name in print is heavenly bliss.

That a small marketplace like Tohri can be featured in a Patna newspaper results in Mathur gaining

tremendous local standing. Despite being the son of a
very wealthy *contractor*, he is extremely honest, hard
working and ambitious. At present, he is collecting
material to write the history of an ancient Kol rebellion
that had occurred in these parts. This will be his *doctoral
thesis.*

Because he roams from village to village to
accumulate material, he knows the catchment area of
the Kuruda river well.

Mathur comes to an arrangement with Peter
Bharati. Peter says—You will give me all the news.
Follow it through to the end. I'll give you five thousand
rupees.

Hearing this, Mathur smiles wryly. He says—My
father is the biggest timber *contractor* in these parts. He
has lots of money. My being a schoolteacher infuriates
him. I won't do this for money.

—Then?

—I have other suspicions about this *daini* business.
I'll certainly do your *reportage*. But when the piece is
published, you will have to acknowledge me in print.

—Certainly.

—My *research* work takes me to those areas anyway,
so you don't have to spend any money; I want the
acknowledgement.

So the deal is struck. Now, a reader of the earlier-
mentioned English magazine may say—But the piece
wasn't in Sharan Mathur's name, was it?

Two things by way of reply.

(One) Why should his name be there? Mathur's
agreement was with Peter Bharati. The piece is credited
to one Kurt Muller. Kurt Muller was under no
agreement to acknowledge Mathur.

(Two) In Mathur's *report*, there was a systematic description of famine–Murhai–Hesadi. The form in which the published article appears has no similarity with Mathur's report at all.

Kurt Muller achieves the impossible.

The torture of witches in *Europe*, and the torture of Jews, Communists and others by Nazis and fascist rulers, fuses with the spine-chilling description of the *daini* hunt; and in his hands the piece turns into a lurid tale.

There were many photographs with the article.

Sevika Aileen Bharati was painted black and dressed up as a *daini* for the photographs. Mathur was wonderstruck at the sight of *roast* chicken in the hands of a *daini* who was supposedly eating the flesh of the *tatui* bird. At the end of the story, the expression in *close-up* on the *daini's* face is so realistic that, on the strength of that one photograph, Aileen Bharati lands the heroine's role in the film, *The Witch*, which is based on the above article. The film will be shot in Arizona in *America*. Because the geography of that area is similar to that of Palamau. A special feature of the film is that all *Bharatiya* characters will be played by whites, and all white-skinned characters by *Bharatiyas*.

Mathur can't even imagine so many possibilities from one event. Trustingly, he does his best to track down the *daini*-story, mounted on his *cycle*.

The next time around, the *daini* is sighted in Hesadi.

The people of Hesadi are at first terribly scared by the *daini* business. Whenever anyone catches sight of his shadow, he fearfully checks to see if it is attached to him. The kith and kin of menstruating and pregnant women mark their movements with suspicion. Black cows, goats and dogs are stoned for their colour. These compulsory rites of the *daini*-terror are scrupulously followed. The *pahaan*, naturally, is wary. He carefully buries the *puja* flowers, wrings the necks of chickens and sprinkles fresh blood everywhere.

When the *daini* is sighted, everyone is relieved. In every village, since it is common to name men and women after the days of the week, there is an abundance of Etowari, Somra–Somna–Soma–Somai–Somri–Somni, Mungla–Mongol–Mungra–Mungli–Mongli, Budhai–Budhna–Budhia–Budhni, Bisra–Birsa–Bisri, Sukia–Sukchar–Sukhni–Sukchari, Sanichar–Sanichari.

Sanichari of Hesadi is currently very busy. She is the midwife of Hesadi village, the one who wards off evil spirits from pregnant women, and the children's doctor as well. So, she has to regularly wander around the jungles in search of roots–herbs–leaves–tubers. All this while, she hadn't entered the jungle for fear of the *daini.*

Her grandson is dear to her. His father and mother left him with his grandmother and died. The boy is just seven years old. He can't help with the household. So Sanichari has been forced to make herself indispensable to village life. Earlier, the *bania* shopkeeper Bhagat did not believe in her abilities. His wife birthed dead sons three times running. Everyone said—This is a job for Sanichari.

Bhagat had to present himself at Sanichari's doorstep. With the waterdrop treatment, the oildrop treatment, and oil massage, Sanichari finally helped

Bhagat's wife with a successful childbirth. The *maroa* or corn she got from Bhagat still sustains her. *Bikhil* or rice is a distant dream for the likes of Sanichari. Only during festivals do they get rice. Their staple diet is the liquid *ghato* made of *bhutta* or *maroa*.

There was a quiet discussion between Sanichari and the *pahaan* about the *daini* business.

Sanichari says—What do you think?

—What do *you* think?

—Think when you're around? You're the *pahaan*. We'll go by whatever you say.

—Why don't you speak first?

Sanichari puts down her bundle of grass. They sell grass to the milkmen of Hesadi *bus junction*. The name of the *bus junction* is also Hesadi, but to Sanichari and the others, it's 'Koha Hesadi' or 'Big Hesadi'. Seven miles to the interior lies their village, the original Hesadi.

Sanichari puts down her bundle and calls to the other women—You go on, I have to talk to the *pahaan*.

—Does the *pahaani* know?

The women laugh and move on. The *pahaan* hands Sanichari a *beedi* and lights one himself.

Sanichari says—What's going on? If the *daini* came from Murhai towards Hesadi, how come we didn't hear her scream? If she went to the Jilad field, how come we didn't hear the ghouls and spirits laughing? Clouds gathered, there was rain—that's not supposed to happen, is it?

The *pahaan* sighed and, stubbing out his *beedi*, tucked the unsmoked half into his waistband. He frowned—If she's a *daini*, why shouldn't we burn her? If we cut her up her blood will spawn other *dainis*. But why shouldn't we burn her?

At this, Sanichari put her hands to her cheeks and stroked them.

The *pahaan* said—You remember?

—Yes, I remember.

—Both of us were raised on my mother's milk. I was a little boy, and you, a tiny girl. Remember?

—I remember. All you used to say was, I'm hungry.

—And you would say, my stomach is still empty. So we, our parents before us, our children after us, have all said the same thing. Your grandson will say the same. But that's not what I'm talking about.

—Your paternal uncle, your *kaka*, became a *dain!* Sanichari said, stroking her cheek.

—They set the house on fire to burn him . . .

—Those flames burnt my cheek. The mark's still there.

—After the *dain* was burnt, it rained, *maroa* flourished, there were fish in the river, all famine fled.

—I don't understand what's going on.

—I think . . .

—What?

Deeply disturbed, the *pahaan* reached for the remaining half of the *beedi*. After the *chakmaki*, coal and so on, he lit up and said—Don't tell anyone. I have a suspicion. The Brahmin *deota* of Tahar cares so deeply for us that if he sees our houses burning, he'll pour *kerosene* on them instead of water. His standard line is, You're lowborn filth, the dust off our shoes. I suspect that he's the one who's started this *daini* business; actually there's no *daini!*

—No *daini!*

—I suspect there isn't.

—But the people of Murhai . . .?

—It was dark. Who knows what they saw? Maybe it was a bear.

—No *daini*!

—I suspect as much. You can feel it, it's not an ill wind, there's nothing scary in the jungle, that dying son of Budhna's recovered miraculously. What kind of *daini* doesn't gobble up children's lives, doesn't hiss into the wind, doesn't frighten away the animals in the forest?

—See for yourself! Do *puja* and see! Do your own calculations. If anyone knows the truth, it'll be you, not us.

—Don't tell anyone.

—No, no.

Sanichari grew very anxious. But gradually she regained her courage. The *pahaan* wouldn't have spoken if he didn't know. There's no *daini*! And if there's no *daini*, why shouldn't she go to the Jilad fields?

With the words 'Jilad fields', that vast, stony waste of enormous rocks came to mind. Between the boulders grew *goli* and *koltuli* plants. Sanichari really needs the roots of the *goli* plant. The sun will set in the evening, its radiance smeared across the monsoon sky. At that time, her hair loose about her shoulders, Sanichari must uproot the *goli*.

This root is the medicine for preventing stillbirth. Bhagat's wife is pregnant again. One child survived. But every time a woman with a history of stillbirth conceives, one has to take precautions.

No one goes to the Jilad field after sunset. In Sanichari's community, they bury their dead, and they also burn corpses on funeral pyres. The practice of funeral pyres began after the Hindus came.

In ancient times, burial was the norm. Stones would be placed on the graves. Those human settlements have ceased to exist. The Jilad field is now an abandoned expanse of burial stones. Everyone knows that when evening falls, the stones awake, rise and walk about.

Sanichari or the *pahaan* can't give in to fear. Sanichari goes there. The roots of the *goli* that grow there are more effective.

The *pahaan* goes there. Every now and then he can sense that the stones are really restless, that the souls of the ancient Oraons are very agitated and disturbed.

That's not surprising. It's not enough to bury the dead. When death enters the family, once the pollution period is over, it is the norm to place water, rice and salt in the burial grounds of one's forefathers. Who can tell where the kinsfolk of the dead buried in the Jilad fields are? But can the spirits be left to shrivel up with hunger in the other world?

That's why the dead souls are disturbed. That's why the *pahaan* has to rush there from time to time. The *pahaan* has a responsibility towards the villagers who are still alive, as well as towards the souls of the dead. The *pahaan* who does not accept this responsibility has no right to be a *pahaan*.

Hence, Sanichari's courage revives after her talk with the *pahaan*. She tells Bhagat's wife—I'll fetch the medicine tomorrow. Clean out your cowshed today, keep the house clean.

—What else will you need?

—Rice, areca nut, oil, the hair of a black she-goat, cow's urine, a new iron key. Bhagat's wife is despairingly weighed down by her womb. She says—Is there a child of iron in my womb, Sanichari? I'm suffering so much.

—Take oil massages, walk about, don't sit around. If you sit around, you'll suffer more later.

—Will I live?

—Of course.

—My brother has sent word that I should be taken to the hospital in town. My husband's not willing.

—They switch babies at the hospital.

—See what you can do.

—Let me see. But don't forget me once mother and child are safely separated.

—I'll give you a ring.

—I don't want a ring. A *bokna* calf.

—Okay. I'll give you one.

Bokna means cow. A cow means a pregnant cow. Sell milk, rear the calf and sell it, make cowdung cakes for fuel. If there's a cow, it'll take care of her grandson's whole life. Thinking along these lines, Sanichari went home and took up her spade. In the late afternoon, she'll get the *goli* roots from the Jilad field.

Her grandson said—I'm hungry.

Sanichari handed him a fistful of corn kernels. Bhagat's wife had given them to her.

On her way to the Jilad field, Sanichari felt that two short sentences would last forever like the sun and the moon. *Kira lagenga*—I'm hungry—and *Malu kular aarguda*—I haven't had enough.

Taka–bede–chando–bilko—the wind, the sky, the moon and stars are forever.

'I'm hungry' and 'I haven't had enough' are also forever. Certainly, in the ancient past, too, no Oraon had ever had enough to fill his stomach. Surely that was how these words had come about.

Sanichari felt that for an old Oraon woman of

Hesadi village, she was about to achieve something great. By pleasing Bhagat's wife and thereby acquiring a *bokna* calf, she was on the verge of securing her grandson's future. .

Was that something to be sneezed at? A cow and cowshed? To sell milk, sell cowdung cakes to Bhagat's wife, sell calves? In a village like Hesadi, an Oraon, after living his entire life, ultimately has nothing to show for all his labour. Except for the stones on his grave. Stones are lifeless, non-living things. Sanichari will leave behind a cow. A cow is a means of making a living.

Lost in happy dreams of a she-calf she was yet to acquire, Sanichari reached the middle of the field. Here, the *monoliths* are close upon one another. It seems as if the two in the centre, tall and towering, are the ancient parents. The other stones are their children. In between the stones, silently flows the Jilad, a branch of the Kuruda river. The earth at the foot of the stones is fertile, watered by the river. There, a dazzling white, flower the *goli* plants.

Sanichari's eyes are blinded by the dark. A tinge of light in the sky, a dark horizon. The darkness is deeper at the foot of the stones. Sanichari is old. Her eyes can only see dimly, even during the day. She saw a spot where the darkness seemed spread out as if someone had poured it on the ground. She began to dig.

Immediately, the *monolith* seems to spring to life, the graveyard seems to roar, the ancient darkness turns into a mis-shapen woman, both hands raised, dishevelled hair flying towards the dimming sky; the darkness screams—*Anh–anh–anh!*

Sanichari was rooted, turned to stone with terror. The *daini* picked up a stone, and, supporting herself with one hand on a large rock, flung it at Sanichari.

How Sanichari managed to flee, she herself doesn't know. Perhaps it is because self-defence is such an inbuilt instinct that, even after seeing the *daini*, she could still drop the shovel, clamber down the rock face, and begin to run.

Footsteps follow her. *Anh–anh–anh!*—the hideous scream rends earth and sky. The gravestones of the ancient Oraons are agitated. Sanichari trips and falls headlong, and, losing consciousness, feels the touch of ghostly fingers on her skin. Then, everything turns dark.

She lies there, and there she would have continued to lie. Strange how coincidences occur. That very evening, Mathur arrives in Hesadi. The *pahaan* is an old friend. He has brought him a bottle of premium liquor, which he hands over. In an adivasi village, someone who is accepted by the *pahaan* is accepted by all.

Mathur says—I'll stay in Koha Hesadi tonight. I have to talk to you.

—I've told you all about the battle between Gidhna Oraon and the English already!

—You haven't told me everything.

—What haven't I told you?

—You are that same Gidhna Oraon's great-great-grandson; you didn't tell me that.

—What's the point in telling you that?

—Why did you conceal it?

The *pahaan's* eyes cloud over, the mistrust towards all non-adivasi people that had been nurtured in his blood now shadowing his eyes.

He said—What's the use of telling you that? Gidhna Oraon was hanged. His brother Kalna was shot dead.

Then my forefathers fled their homes. Should I invite
death by telling you all this?

—Why are you scared of telling me, now?

—We're always scared, all the time. You won't
understand. Why talk so much? Drink. You've brought
beedis, give me one.

—One more thing.

—What?

—Send for Sanichari. Didn't she say she had
information about *dainis* and ghouls?

—She'll be here soon.

—Where's she gone?

—To the Jilad field.

—Isn't she afraid of the *daini?*

The *pahaan*'s eyes grew cunning and wary. He
said—Perhaps she's not afraid of the *daini.*

Mathur stared straight ahead and said in an
indifferent tone—Perhaps there is no *daini.* Perhaps
Hanuman Misra has let this *daini* story loose to avenge
some old grievance.

Brahmin! *Deota! Police officer, MLA,* everyone stays at
his place, sits at his feet. The other day a saheb came all
the way from Patna. How can he, of all people, spread
tall tales like that?

Now both of them laughed. The *pahaan* said—
You're a cunning jackal! You're trying to make me put
your thoughts into words.

—Are you any less a jackal?

—The things you say!

—Let's have a drink.

—Let Sanichari come.

But Sanichari did not come. On enquiry, it was
learnt that she hadn't returned. The *pahaan* said—Then

we must go in search of her. Could she have tripped and fallen on the stones?

No one wants to go to the Jilad field after dark. Finally, the *pahaan* and Mathur set out.

They are the ones who come upon the unconscious Sanichari lying on the sandy banks of the Jilad river. Someone has clawed the skin on her back. Footprints on the sand. Both of them are startled and Mathur says—I'll carry her on my back. You walk ahead with the *torch*.

As they finish talking, a laugh rings out from the spot where the Jilad and Kuruda meet. An eerie, inhuman sound in that atmosphere. Immediately after the laugh comes the earth-rending '*Anh–anh–anh!*' The disbelief and anxious fear in the minds of the *pahaan* and Mathur now finds an explanation. In this way, Mathur becomes involved as an eyewitness in the *daini* affair.

Later, the *pahaan* and Mathur could not remember how they carried Sanichari back. That scream and the laughter pursued them. Mathur frequently had the urge to put Sanichari down, turn back and shine the *torch*. But at the moment, the unconscious Sanichari is the *top priority*.

In the village, she is laid down in the *pahaan*'s house. The *pahaan* takes the responsibility of caring for her. Mathur sees how even the sceptical *pahaan*, in the wink of an eye, has become a great believer in the omnipotence of Hanuman Misra.

The *pahaan* curses himself and says—I didn't understand a thing.

—What should you have understood?

—There *was* a *daini*.

Mathur is seized with the desire to go off alone, *torch* in hand, to look for the *daini*. But now, circumstances have changed. Terror grips these people and drives them to embark on *daini*-hunting like a violent, barbaric army.

There are a few rituals that govern the terror of the *daini*. Check whether your shadow is stuck to you or not, mark the movements of menstruating and pregnant women with suspicion, if you see a black cow or dog, stone it to see whether it changes its form.

Don't answer if anyone calls you at night. If a dust-eddy rises in an odd place, beware of the wind. Don't speak within hearing of kites–crows–vultures. They're messengers of the *daini*. Be careful with children. Young blood is the *daini's* favourite food.

There are rules for *daini* hunting, too.

His face hardened with resolve, the *pahaan* strikes the *nagara*. On the hide of the *nagara*, on the *pahaan's* leather-bound *nagara*, the danger alarm can be awesome, can quake the heart.

The *nagara* is sounded. Men begin to collect. In their hands, burning *mashaals,* their waistcloths heavy with stones. Women pick up the children and bolt the doors. No one looks accusingly at the *pahaan*. The *pahaan's* face is agonized. His resolve unwavering. His eyes sharp.

Mathur's *report* to Peter Bharati—As soon as all the men of the village had assembled, we set out under the leadership of the *pahaan*. A strange drama was taking place before my eyes. I was not able to take part. This was an internal affair. A caste Hindu, an outsider, I walked along as a spectator.

There is a forest beyond the confluence of the Jilad

and Kuruda. A dense forest. At one time, the Forest Department, finding the earth suitable, had planted *khair* trees. *Khair* trees grow very fast and quickly fill up all the open spaces between the other trees.

However, the aim of planting these *khair* trees, which was to develop a cottage industry in order to improve the condition of the local adivasis, was not achieved. The Forest Department realized there was no profit in it, after covering costs.

The sand bore 'the *daini*'s footprints. We followed the footprints across the river. Shouting, the men advance, burning *mashaals* in hand. The *pahaan* leads. Arms raised, unarmed, he calls aloud as he walks. He is extremely disturbed. Sanichari is his milk-sister.

—There! screams the *pahaan* and stops. We saw, upon stopping we saw, something rocking to and fro on a boulder in front of us.

I thought it was a bear. Bears can stand on two legs. Their claws are very sharp. The wounds I had seen on Sanichari's back were made by very sharp claws. To tell the truth, I had not completely dismissed the possibility of it being a bear.

But the thing that rose upon the stone was not a bear. Its screaming rent the sky. The way an ox shrieks *anh–anh–anh!* when branded by a hot iron. But it was a human voice. With the screaming, a furious roar. Then it began to hurl stones.

The men were dropping their *mashaals* and fleeing. The *pahaan* said—It'll devour the life of anyone who flees now. No one is to run away. They chased her out of Murhai. It's our turn now.

They brandished their *mashaals*, ran forward with desperate courage, and began to hurl stones. This time they followed the rules of *daini*-hunting laid down by Hanuman Misra of Tahar. Stone the *daini* to chase it away. Stones will fix these *dainis* good and proper. It will be catastrophic if *daini* blood is shed, disastrous if she dies.

In the light of the *mashaals*, they returned to the stone age. I was a twentieth-century spectator at that stone-age battle, where stones were weapons. This battle was mine as well. One had to fight to survive. But in my heart of hearts, I could not join them, try as I might. At this moment, with this battle, I recognized what a self-serving, *doctorate*-greedy human being I, too, was. People like me stand apart and, even after watching the battle, note the facts and reasons to construct theories out of them.

As the battle of stones continued, the fact of a group of people attacking one person began to feed the thirst for revenge in them all. I began to smell the keen, cruel vengeance that terror had spawned. The smell of *violence.*

At intervals, they would toss their *mashaals* into the sky. In the reddish, flickering light of the *mashaals*, suddenly I saw the *daini*'s distended, mis-shapen figure. Dark, naked, young, the distorted outlines of a body.

Once she had run out of stones, she descended the rock-face, screaming—*Anh–anh–anh*! They hurl stones with desperate force. Not pebbles, large stones. If these hit her head, the *daini's* blood will flow. But who amongst them cares to remember this?

The *daini* began to run towards the forest. *Anh–anh–anh*! that terrible scream. They give chase. They hound her into the forest, they return. I remain behind, standing.

Returning, the *pahaan* said—No sleep tonight. She'll suck the blood of anyone who sleeps. All of you come to my house. Bring liquor, whatever you have at home. Drink, carouse the night away, stay awake. Tomorrow we'll do a *puja.*

This is exactly what had happened at Murhai village. There, too, the villagers had spent the whole night awake at the *pahaan's* command. That same night, two lovers from that village had eloped. That, too, they say, was due to the *daini's* curse. Because those who eloped were the first to spot the *daini.*

We came back. They distil their own liquor. There's toddy in every home. They also make *tonk,* a very potent intoxicant.

While everyone caroused through the night, the *pahaan* told me a true story about *dainis.*

On the verandah of the *pahaan's* house sit Mathur and the *pahaan.* At a distance, the men and women of the village drink the night away. Chasing off the *daini* gives rise to a kind of victorious glee. The people of Murhai had felt it; so do they. Now, they are singing to keep awake. A song sung at Holi. Holi is the day on which their annual hunt is held. They sing,

> On Holi he went to hunt
> The boy after my own heart
> Oh, did he go east?
> Oh, did he go west?
> Evening falls, the Holi fires are lit
> Why hasn't he come back?
> Shameless I am, I stand on Kuruda's banks,
> When he returns with the hunted deer
> I'll share the load,
> (For) Won't he be weary when he returns?

Mathur was listening to the song thoughtfully. He had come here with a particular mindset. What he has seen makes him think differently about the people of Hesadi. Whether the *daini* business is true or false, the people's terror, and the anger and violence born of that terror, are undeniably true. Even truer is the matter of Hanuman Misra. It has been proved that his orders are unquestioningly obeyed by the non-Hindu adivasis as well. All earth crumbles away. But the earth on which Hanuman Misra's supremacy is founded is gradually hardening into *granite*.

The *daini* was no less violent. Why? Is she really a *daini*? It is generally known that *dainis* are defeated by certain elements, like iron or fire. Are *dainis* also defeated by stones? This is a new chapter in the *daini*-scriptures. *Dainis* are also finished off by killing. Even now, anyone suspected of being a *daini* is killed.

What does a *daini* do? She casts an evil eye from afar, or uses her evil magic to curdle milk, kill cows–goats, destroy crops, bring drought, cause famine, take the lives of little children, lure menstruating women into her coils, enter the wombs of pregnant women.

Are these the only people who believe in the *daini*? Mathur's mother doesn't serve food to her children or let them eat in front of outsiders, she says the evil eye will be cast upon them. When Mathur's wife or sisters are pregnant, she doesn't allow them to come out into the courtyard at dusk with their hair untied. She says— The ill wind will get them.

Mathur accepts these things in his daily life. He himself has an MA degree. His own brothers are BA and BL pass. Not only by Tohri standards, they're a very educated family by the standards of the entire region.

To top it all, Mathur's father is a very big timber *contractor.* Many *lorries,* an enormous godown, a factory for splitting logs.

Who casts the evil eye upon their house? Who sends the ill wind? Doesn't belief in such things mean an underlying belief in the *daini?* So, there is a class of *daini* that keeps even a family like theirs on tenterhooks?

Mathur was ruminating upon all this, and the realization that, in his educated mind, learning was merely a surface layer with the darkness of superstition beneath, was making him despair.

The *pahaan* said—You don't believe in *dain-daini.* But human beings do turn into *dainis.* I'll tell you a tale from my own life.

—Go ahead.

—You were asking about Gidhna Oraon. The Gidhna who fought the English was my ancestor. Now, we have nothing. Like everyone else, I too work on the land of Golbadan of Koha Hesadi at harvest time, and at other times, do whatever work I can get. Plus this work as *pahaan.*

—Which is good work!

—It's neither bad nor good, it's work.

—Carry on.

—Another Gidhna was born. Into our family. My father's brother. I wonder why his parents named him Gidhna. After Gidhna Oraon, no one in this family keeps that name anymore. I grew up in the lap of this uncle. A tiger killed my father, you know that. My *kaka* was a very good man.

Till he made a young man of me, he was a good man. *Kaka's* wife was a bitch, she got her brother to send off both their sons to the Ramgarh coal mines. That broke my *kaka's* heart.

In coal, there's hard cash to be made. When a new owner bought off the coal mine, *Kaka's* sons took a room in a *pucca* house. *Kaka's* wife left the village, and went off to live with her sons.

That's when the good man turned bad. I told him— I never knew my *baap*, I only have you. You stay with me. He said—I won't eat up your rice. I said—That's fine, eat your own rice, but stay with me.

You know what he said? He said, I won't live with the *deota*. I've always obeyed the *deo-deota*. And I'm being punished like this in my old age. You're fourteen now, you'll be the next *pahaan*, that's why the *pahaan* has adopted you.

Kaka kept to himself, I led my own life. That year, it rained very heavily. The Jilad was in flood, the Kuruda was in flood, rushing furiously like a mad elephant. The *pahaan* said to me, You're still short, a little boy, can you go and find out what your *kaka* is up to when he lights a lamp at night?

I see that *kaka* lights his lamp and calls out to someone—Serve the rice! Bring me some water! Fetch the *moua*. Don't go away and leave me alone.

I say—*Kaka*? Who're you calling?

Kaka says—Your *kaki*. I saw that he'd drunk a lot of *moua*.

I told the *pahaan*. The *pahaan* thought deeply. Finally he said—He goes out at night, returns at dawn, what's happened to him?

I say, I don't know! I work like the devil in your household all day long, and fall asleep at dusk.

Soon after this, people began to die one after the

other. The *pahaan's* wife hurt her leg on a brick. Then, she became bent like a bow, foamed at the mouth, and died. Bhagat's paternal aunt, his *pishi*, drowned in the Kuruda waters. And who could tell what happened to the children? They hiccupped, their limbs stiffened, they died. After seven–eight deaths, the *pahaan* called everyone and showed them that *kaka* left his house at night, went to the Jilad field, returned at dawn. Each time he went to the field, someone died.

Mathur had been listening with bated breath. He said—Then? What happened after that?

—He was tried.

—Tried!

The *pahaan* tried him. *Kaka* said, Yes, I go to the Jilad field. The *deo-deotas* did not give me justice. I ask the ghouls and spirits, Whose fault was it that my wife went away, that my sons don't ask after me, that I'm dying alone and hungry? The *pahaan* said, Your nephew wanted to support you, why don't you stay with him? *Kaka* said, I'm poor. I can't look after him, his *kaki* didn't give him enough to eat, I gave him to you, you adopted him. He's now your son. He'll be the next *pahaan*. How can I stay with him and arrange for my own food? And besides, when I see *deo-deota puja*, it makes me furious.

It struck Mathur that these were the agonized words of a deeply unfortunate man.

—That the worship of the gods made him furious explained it all. After that . . .

—What happened?

—At night, everyone piles a mound of dry branches outside *kaka's* door. I can neither act nor speak. My heart flutters like a pigeon flapping its wings.

The *pahaan* took swift, deep drags of his *beedi*. The past still agitates him.

—Then they lit the fire. As the flames leapt up, *kaka* screamed. Hearing the scream I tried to push through the fire and enter, but everyone held me back. A tongue of flame licked Sanichari's cheek; the mark's still there.

—Then?

—All the curses on the village vanished.

—Then?

—The police came. No one said anything. They pitched tents in the village, investigated for a day or two, feasted on chicken and *moua*, and left.

—*Kaka's* wife and sons?

—Who knows where they are?

—All this happened long ago.

—Of course.

—The night's almost ended.

—There's a lot of work today.

—There'll be a *puja*?

—We must offer *puja*.

— The *daini* won't ever come to Hesadi again?

— No. We must see to it that she doesn't. The boys of the village don't listen to anyone. They take the cows and goats to the fields. The goats piss and shit on the grave stones. It isn't right.

—Lie down for a while.

—You too.

Lying on a grass mat, on the verandah, Mathur now heard what the boy in the Holi song had to say.

> O, girl, oh girl with a heart of stone,
> I've come back from the hunt—
> You're not there at the edge of the forest.
> You're not there on the outskirts of the village.

Why have you come with wet feet,
Feet wet from Kuruda waters.
Have you found another mate,
A *kusum* flower in your hair
And your face all flushed?

Mathur went to sleep. Before he fell asleep, he said to the *pahaan*—I'll come back again after a trip to Tohri. I must find out what happened to the *daini*.

After the incident in Hesadi village, one day, three old men came together at the big market in Koha Hesadi.

The *pahaans* of Kuruda, Hesadi and Murhai. The *pahaan* of Murhai said—That Sanichari of yours died, did she?

—Yes.

—Died in hospital!

—Mathur took her.

—What did the doctor say?

—It seems she had some disease. A disease in which wounds don't heal, the blood won't stop flowing.

—The blood didn't stop flowing?

—No. The blood kept oozing out, she was covered with sores. Her eyes sank into hollows.

The Kuruda *pahaan* couldn't bear to look at the grief-stricken, agonized face of the Hesadi *pahaan*. He said—Baba! What does the doctor know? Doctors only know how to give injections, make you swallow medicines, shove pipes up your nose. Death stuck its claws into Sanichari. Can a human being survive that? Sanichari's suffering is over, good.

—Her grandson?

—He's with me. She was my milk-sister. He's a little

boy! Where'll he stay?

—Her house?

—Let it collapse.

—She knew a lot about medicines and mantras.

—That's what killed her.

The *pahaan* of Hesadi said—Somra, it's getting dark. Tell us why you've summoned us.

—What's there to say? No sign of the *daini*. That's even more frightening. Should we wait until she shows herself before we beat her to pulp? I suggest, and our boys are ready, why don't we all get together and hunt her out!

The *pahaan* of Hesadi says softly—No. Our boys will also be willing, but give it a second thought.

—You tell us. You're our senior in age, knowledge and respect.

The *pahaan* of Hesadi knew that the respect shown to him by these two loincloth-clad, shrivelled-skinned old men just like him was because his forefathers were Gidhna and Kalna Oraon. Everyone knows the song about Gidhna's hanging and Kalna's murder.

Gidhna, you were not scared.

You put the noose around your own neck.

Kalna, you were not scared

You walked forward to take the bullet.

Your names have become the leaves on the trees,

Which only fall to grow again, anew.

He said—Each of those boys is someone's son. The touch of the *daini* will kill us. How can we, as *pahaans*, send our own sons to be killed?

—No, you're right.

—Let's act when the time comes. Now for the good

news: Golbadan's going to run the *colliery?*

—So I hear.

—Let's see. It's so difficult to survive.

Golbadan got a bargain when he bought the *colliery.*
His brother's brick kiln is shut down, too.

—They've closed down out of sheer mischief.

The *pahaan* of Murhai now fidgets and says—My son
has heard that the *colliery* and brick kiln have been
bought by Hanuman Misra of Tahar. He'll begin
operations in the month of *Poush.*

—Let him buy it. Whoever buys it won't pay us more
than twelve annas a day. Will they? If we get work, we'll
take it.

—What times these are. No rain at the proper time,
no nip in the air.

—It'll get worse.

—But we must try. We must tell the Adivasi Office to
ensure that we get work as coolies.

The *pahaan* of Hesadi told Mathur this. He said—
Why don't you talk to the officer at Tohri!

—I shall.

These *surface collieries* are a special characteristic of
the region. Here, low-grade coal lies close to the surface
of the earth. Nationalization has not been able to bring
the small *surface collieries* scattered in these remote areas
under government control. In defiance of the *sarkar,*
these *collieries* flourish unchecked under private
ownership.

·In '70-71, the same people who raised the slogan
that industry was threatened in West Bengal, entered
south-east Bihar, and at that time bought these *collieries*
for only ten or fifteen thousand each. Adivasi and local
lowcaste coolies come as cheap as water. They mine the

coal with shovels, spades, even forks. *Trucks* carry this
coal far, far away over *kuccha* roads.

Brick kilns are also very profitable. Even houses of
unbaked local bricks last many years, to say nothing of
baked bricks. This brick-earth can be found only around
the *collieries.* An individual can become the owner of a
colliery by spending just ten or fifteen or thirty thousand.
If you mine coal for just ten years, there's a huge profit.
The local labourers consider twelve annas a day a boon,
because in no other line of work can they earn so much
money.

Mathur made enquiries and learnt that it was true.
Hanuman Misra of Tahar was not satisfied with merely
constructing a temple. He had bought up many
orchards, a lot of land. Buying a *colliery* or two will
deliver up the region securely into his hands.

Hanuman Misra admitted as much to him. He said
remorsefully—These are the negative results of learning
English. My sons no longer want to involve themselves
with the temple. Look at yourself! Did you go into your
father's line of work? I'm compelled to do all this for
their sake. I say, Go, do what you will. Why one, go buy
up ten *collieries.* I'm quite content with my temple.

—You'll employ local *labour,* won't you?

—I want to. Let's see what Vishwanathji ordains.
Nothing will happen without his blessings.

Mathur came back to Hesadi and reported
everything. Then he said—The brick kiln is in ruins. It
has to be built afresh.

—Did you go to see it?

—No! It's too far away.

—There's a cave three villages after Hesadi, the
brick kiln is beyond that.

—In Tura village?

—Near Tura. Tura is a little further ahead.

—Is it true that you find deer there?

—You want to hunt?

—Just asking.

—I don't know. Who goes that far? And the area around the cave isn't safe.

—Why?

—It's dangerous at night.

—There's no sign of the *daini*.

—What am I to think, tell me? There was no way of knowing that the *daini* was there. Poor Sanichari died. Even thinking of it makes me sad.

—Come on, let's go hunting.

—Hunting!

—I'll get guns. A *permit* for hunting?

—Oh! The number of *permits* you people need.

—All the *sarkari* laws are totally groundless. A leopard enters the village, kills cows and goats. Should we wait for a *permit* to kill it? A huge *gulbagha* leopard like that, what does it know of *permits*?

—That's true. You're really keen on it?

—Yes.

—How well do you shoot? *Champion.*

—We'll see. This *gulbagha* is very dangerous. The village dogs are our sentries. They're the village police. And if the *gulbagha* can get hold of a dog, it wants nothing else. So that's why I'll kill it.

—The dog?

—*Gulbagha.*

—Very well! Can you bring some *kerosene* the next time you come? You can't get *kerosene* on *permit* in Koha Hesadi. *Moua* oil smokes a lot, it makes the eyes smart.

—Okay. I won't be able to ride my *cycle* from Tohri, in that case. Send a couple of boys.

A few days later, two boys arrive at Tohri. They'll carry two tins of *kerosene*. Some rope and nails. The *pahaan* had sent a message asking Mathur to bring some red medicine. Only Mathur knows this medicine which heals wounds and burns. Sanichari's grandson has been scalded by hot water.

Finally, they said—The *pahaan* has asked you to bring a gun and bullets.

—Why? Where's the *gulbagha*?

—In the jungle around Dhai village.

—Who's seen it?

—Who can spot it? Three dogs have disappeared from the village one after the other. Vultures are circling above the jungle.

Mathur took a large bottle of *mercurochrome*. This is a habit of the *pahaan's*. He has no faith in doctors, medicines, or injections, but the medicine that Mathur carries in his bag, *mercurochrome*, had healed the blister on his foot, and he hasn't forgotten that. It seemed to Mathur that though the *pahaan* had a different mentality, yet he was beginning to accept the superiority of science, albeit in minute, atomic proportions. Once Mathur had made him take *antibiotics* for the *sepsis* in his teeth. The *pahaan* had been the most hopeful that Sanichari would survive if she was taken to hospital.

Perhaps, some day, the *pahaan* will give indications of rational thinking in the matter of the *daini*, as well.

But is rational thinking effective in the matter of the *daini*? Is Mathur any closer to fathoming the *daini* affair by virtue of his own education and learning?

After some thought, Mathur tells his wife—Give me

some of Dilip's old clothes.

—I was going to trade them for utensils.

—No.

Even after a couple of kids, Mathur's relationship with his wife is very cordial. Mira never nags him for teaching instead of joining his father's business. She is a gentle, calm person. Because her husband is a misfit in the family, she feels a kind of motherly affection for him.

Carrying a bundle of clothes, *mercurochrome*, ropes, nails and *beedis*, Mathur sets off. Gun and bullets. He is very fond of hunting. Before setting off he notices that Mira's face is pale. She must be fasting for some ritual.

—Are you fasting?

—Yes.

—Why?

—I'll offer *puja*.

—For what?

—For you.

—Why?

—Isn't the *daini* there? Where you're going?

—How can the *daini* harm me when I have someone like you at home?

—Don't say that. Just come back safely. That saheb is the root of all the trouble. He himself is sitting pretty in Patna, and he's pushed you into the fire.

—No Mira, I'll get my *doctorate* and take you away to America.

When he said this, he possibly harboured some such dream. In a few days, his mentality underwent a complete change, as if a landslide had wiped out his dreams, rendering them unreal in the face of a wounding blow from harsh reality. Now, after everything is over, Mathur no longer cherishes such dreams. He is still teaching in Tohri, and goes often to Hesadi with the excuse of collecting spicy titbits about Gidhna and the history of their rebellion for a *thesis* he is never going to write. He has developed a soft corner for the *pahaan* and the curious reader will be glad to know that even now their feelings for each other run parallel, a river beside a railway line. There is no chance of their meeting. Mathur and *pahaan* are like the river and the railway line, if they meet at some point, disaster is inevitable.

Mathur goes off to Hesadi. Applies medicine on Sanichari's grandson's blisters. Nails together a wooden perch for the courtyard. Distributes *kerosene* to everyone in the village along with the *pahaan* and earns their gratitude. And the next morning, after having promised to shoot the leopard and take a photograph of the villagers surrounding its carcass, he sets off for Dhai with a few youths in tow.

Three villages beyond Hesadi, there's a cave. Then the brick kiln. Then Tura village. Tura is a Munda village.

The farthest of the three villages is Dhai. Dhai is a tiny village. On the banks of the Kuruda river. On the opposite bank is the jungle. A jungle of *amloki, palash, sidha* and *shishu* trees. The village dogs regularly frequent the river bank. The frequent disappearance of the dogs means a leopard. Everyone knows that leopards love dog meat. Vultures circling above the jungle indicate that the half-eaten carcasses must be lying there. Mathur tells the boys—Not a word. Leopards are very dangerous. They'll run away if they hear a single sound. He's excited. It feels good to walk cautiously through the jungle. Dim green shadows of the deep jungle, fun to walk through. One hopes there are no snakes. As long as they don't bite the feet.

Then the forest thins out. A few storm-felled trees.

Sitting on a tree stump, her back to them, the *daini* lifts a hand.

Raises the leg of a dog to her mouth. A hammer pounds Mathur's chest. The youths run helter-skelter.

The *daini* turns her face. Then, rending the forest with her scream—*anh–anh–anh!*—she stands up. A distended, grotesque figure. Mathur covers his eyes, drops his gun, turns back. Then runs.

Running, he looks back. The *daini* is giving chase. But slowly. Mathur keeps running.

The boys had assumed that Mathur had been killed by the *daini*. The *daini*'s scream, *Anh–anh–anh!* confirmed this. Mathur is a fast runner and is able to catch up with them.

Mathur says—It's not a *daini*. It's a human being. They pooh-poohed him. Terror, total terror. And with it, vengeful violence.

They sprinted through Dhai village shouting— *Daini! Daini!* Women, go indoors, men get ready, we're coming!

They went to Hesadi. The males of Dhai, Topa and Burudi villages gathered. Now Mathur cannot quietly slip off stage in this drama. Yet it is not his drama, he has no role to play. He waits.

While waiting, listening to their angry conversation, he suddenly discovers an explosive truth.

That's why clouds wander about the sky, but there's no rain! No tubers grow in the forests. No fish in the river. The wind seems to pant and sigh!

It's like this. Suddenly Mathur understood. These people have no niche in the man-made economic cycle. Brick kiln–*colliery*–Bokaro steel–timber industry–railroad–crops, fields—everything has made them redundant—

Nature is their only hope. If it rains, crops grow, the forest flourishes, roots and tubers are available, there are fish in the river. Nature's breasts are dry with no rain. So they hold the *daini* responsible, and are angry. The people of Bharat don't want them. If nature, too, turns away, they will be wiped out.

One by one, men gather. Each one is armed. Each one carries a stick. Stones in their waistcloths.

Mathur understands why they're angry. Despite this knowledge, he won't be able to meet them as an equal on their mental plane. Like them, he is a local boy. But Mathur holds the *butt* of the gun in his hands. It's barrel aims at their chests. Caste Hindu versus adivasi. It is impossible for the killer to drop the gun, link hands and become one with the *target*.

It was eleven before the *pahaan* of Hesadi arrived. Then, over a hundred people entered the forest yelling and screaming in unison.

The *daini* stands up. She doubles over, then limps forward. She stumbles again and again. It's fruitless to throw stones in the jungle. The trees trap them. *Anh–anh–anh!* The howl is at times a roar, at times an agonized scream.

—*Hey*! Wait, all of you. She's crossing the river.
—Where's she going?
—*Arrey, arrey*, she's going into the cave.
—The cave!
—Look, everyone!

Leaving the shelter of the jungle, the *daini* crosses the river. Slowly. She turns her face from side to side. Throws up her hands, then clutches her stomach. Her walk, her movements, are strange.

—Stone her!

—Make sure she doesn't bleed.

The *daini* stoops. Picks up a stone and turns.

The people stop short. Mathur is behind them. He can't see properly. Suddenly, almost at lightning speed, the *daini* bolts, as though desperate, into the cave.

—There, there, there she goes!

Everyone gathers in front of the cave. The Mundas of Tura village have come, too. The mood is vengeful, violent.

The *pahaan* of Dhai village says—What have you done?

—What have we done?

—She's entered our very life!

—Did we force her to?

—She'll never come out of the cave.

—How were we to know?

—You can't leave us in this danger! We won't let you go.

—How will you stop us?

—We'll cut you to pieces!

—You think we can't hit back?

The *pahaan* of Hesadi said—This is senseless talk. We're in danger!

—Tell us what to do.

—She must be brought out and chased off.

—Who'll do it?

—We will.

—How?

—What do you do to a fox in a hole?

—Smoke it out?

—Smoke her out.

The *pahaan* of Dhai said—Burn her to death? Is that
what you're saying? You'll burn her?

—No, no, we don't want to die because we killed
her.

—Then what are you suggesting?

—Light a fire at the mouth of the cave. The smoke
and the heat will force her out. Then hound her off.

The *pahaan* of Tura said—Head her off into the
jungle, not the village. Our village is already suffering.
These are bad times!

—Who isn't suffering?

—That's what I'm saying.

What Mathur sees now is totally unreal. With
amazing swiftness, with terrible violence, they cut down
trees and bushes. With the ordered precision of
soldiers, these bloodthirsty people pile the bushes and
branches at the mouth of the cave. Someone from Dhai
village fetches *kerosene*, pours it on. The *pahaan* of
Hesadi strikes a *chakmaki*.

Fire, fire. The wind breathes out. The fire grows.
Smoke fills the cave. Green branches snap loudly in the
flames. The people step back from the heat.

They all crane their necks. Everyone is still. Glee on
every face. Deep resolve.

—Come out! Come out.

Why is the *pahaan* of Hesadi swaying? Is he chanting
mantras? Is this the rule for smoking out a *daini*?

Everyone sways. Everyone chants—Come out! Come
out! Come out! Is Mathur himself swaying together with
these people? Does the Stone Age exist somewhere

deep within him, too? Mathur clutches a branch to force his body back under control.

—*Hui! Hui,* look there!

The swirls of smoke suddenly coil like a snake, and slither slowly into the cave like a python. Everything is dark with smoke.

Anh–anh–anh–anh–anh!—the shriek, the scream, a human cry, after all it's human beings who turn into *dainis.* When this happens, other humans smoke it out. Why is Mathur's heart breaking?

Anh–anh–anh–anh! Suddenly, the screams stop. Silence. An awful silence. Then agonized wails. Strange and unbelievable. As if a newborn child is crying.

Everyone is terrorized, distraught. Suddenly, the *pahaan* of Tura tore apart the unreal scene with his scream—Naa-aah!

He runs forward. Drags up a large branch. Swipes the flames with both hands. He's clearing a path.

—What are you doing?

—Let me go.

—No!

—I have to, I must!

—No.

—Let me go.

—You'll die.

—I'm dying anyway, I'm as good as dead. *Ha,* I throw myself at your feet—

The *pahaan* of Tura sank his teeth into the restraining hand. The man let go. He is bleeding.

The *pahaan* wipes his blood-smeared mouth with the palm of his hand and says—I'll kill anyone who goes forward. Everyone is stunned, puzzled.

He runs in through the flames. Then the cave cries

out in his voice—Somri! Somri! Somri!

Mathur comes forward. Returns to reality from an unreal nightmare. He looks at the assembled crowd, steps over the flames and enters.

Eyes blinded by the darkness of the cave. Stench of bats. Crazed by the smoke, hordes of bats flap and reel.

On the floor of the cave kneels the *pahaan*. A naked young woman is lying there. Between her legs, still connected by the umbilical cord, is the newborn infant.

—My daughter!

The *pahaan* of Tura addresses the floor. Then, lifting his eyes in the darkness—She's dumb! She can't speak. Her body grew, but not her brain! I sent her to the household of Hanuman Misra in Tahar, to work in the cowshed. In the cowshed.

—When?

—A year ago. For the last five months there's been no news of her. Misraji says she's gone away, who knows where? I've searched high and low, I haven't been able to find her. Later I learnt the *thakur's* son had spoilt her. I went to ask, and got a shoe in my face. *Daini, daini,* the *thakur* spread these stories about a *daini*! I never knew my Somri was the *daini*! I never knew!

—She's not a *daini*!

Mathur turns. The *pahaans* of Hesadi and Murhai.

The *pahaan* of Tura shakes his head like a trapped animal. Then, in a breathless, distorted voice, says—Kill me too. And this baby as well.

—Not a *aaini*!

These are the only words the *pahaan* of Hesadi speaks in this connection. That is, his last words on the subject of the *daini*. Thereafter, the *pahaan* of Hesadi's words are the first spoken in connection with Somri, the daughter of the *pahaan* of Tura.

—Please come out. Go call the women, this is their business.

—What business?

The *pahaan* of Tura raises his dazed, befuddled eyes. What business can those about to be slaughtered have? The *pahaan* of Hesadi clutches the walls of the cave and looks away. Says—Aren't there any women in Dhai village? To cut the umbilical cord? Call them. Get up.

Tells Mathur—Take off your shirt. Hand it to her father. Her father may stay here, you and I can't.

The *pahaan* of Hesadi comes out. Calls out—We'll talk about this later. Somri, the slow-witted, voiceless daughter of the *pahaan* of Tura, has birthed a son. Someone go to the village, call the women. *Pahaan!* Is there no one in your village?

—Where's the *daini?*

—Go ask in Tahar. They got their son to rape the dumb, slow-witted girl and threw her out. Then they spread the *daini* alarm, saying, don't kill her, just stone her.

—What are you saying?

—What I'm saying is true. This is the grandson of the grandson of Gidhna–Kalna. Would I have said this about a *daini?* Go, go to the village!

There is nothing more to say. Gidhna–Kalna are the dreams that live in everyone's blood, let them be.

The *pahaan* of Hesadi never invokes their names. If he ever does, every single Oraon is bound to obey him, even though he is as poor and hungry as they are.

The Munda youths of Tura rush towards the village.

The women come from Dhai. They cut the umbilical cord, clean the baby. They who had wanted to stone the *daini* and drive her away, who had tried to smoke her out of the cave, now cut branches to make a *machaan*.

The women carried Somri out. Mathur's *shirt* covered her nakedness. Somri's eyes looked at them all. No, there's no vengeance in their eyes. The men could not even look at her.

They laid her, along with the child, on the *machaan*. The *pahaani* of Dhai village spread a grass mat on it. They were lifted up. The *pahaan* of Tura walked alongside the *machaan*, with a leafy branch to shield her from the sun.

The men broke up. Each to return to his own village. The *pahaan* of Hesadi and Mathur entered the jungle. Mathur found his gun and the bullets.

Walking along, Mathur didn't say a word. The *pahaan* of Hesadi said two things. Hunger drove her to eat raw flesh.

Mathur said nothing.

—Whatever you said to Hanuman Misra no longer holds good. We won't work as coolies for him. Won't let anyone work. Won't allow outside coolies in, either.

Mathur inclined his head in agreement without a word. Peace, a wonderful peace. The *pahaan* of Hesadi would look around at intervals, amazed, as if he was seeing things for the first time. Mathur could sense that he had realized the wind was as fragrant, the forest as green, as before. Because the oppressive cloud of terror had dissolved, the *pahaan* knew in his heart that everything was as before. The colour of the sky had never changed. The wind had never stopped blowing. Nature was exactly as she had always been in a dry year. It was only because the *pahaan* had changed that everything seemed to have changed, too.

The *pahaan* repeated—We won't work. Won't let any outsiders work, either.

Mathur said nothing. He nodded his head in agreement. His eyes were brimming with tears. The *pahaan* said—Why're you crying?

Mathur said nothing. There's no point at which he and the *pahaan* can meet. They run parallel to each other. They'll never meet—how can he explain why he feels like crying?

They leave the jungle and descend to the breast of the river. If they had looked back, they would have been able to see the brass pennant on Hanuman Misra's towering temple in far-away Tahar.

They do not look back. They still have a long way to walk.

salt

NOT BY HAND, OR BY BREAD, *nimak se marega*—I'll kill you by salt, Uttamchand Bania had said. He was the *bania*, the trader—he was also the *mahajan*, the moneylender; and for many generations, his family had ruled the Jhujhar *belt*. That the local Oraon and Kol peoples would say 'no' to him was unimaginable.

But the unimaginable did occur. In the reign of this *sarkar*. Before this, *sarkars* had come and *sarkars* had gone, but nothing like this had ever happened.

Jhujhar is an adivasi village in the lap of the Palamau Reserve Forest. The villagers are allowed to graze cattle and goats in the forest, and pick sticks and twigs off the forest floor for firewood. They can also take leaves to thatch their huts. Apart from this, they steal bamboo, tubers and tamarind leaves. The Forest Department turns a blind eye. They kill the odd porcupine, rabbit or bird. The census of these forest creatures and birds is not totally accurate. Hence, the Forest Department keeps its eyes shut about this as well. But they rarely manage to snare any meat. Because the animals are now too alert. They can't be trapped easily.

The village is in the lap of the Reserve Forest. A strip of land crowding the bank of the Koel river. The land, however, belongs to Uttamchand. After the Kol rebellion of 1831, the Hindu traders who re-entered this area were Uttamchand's forefathers. One of them bought up the adivasis' fertile jungle land hand over fist. In those days, like today, it was very easy to buy land and drive out the adivasis. Adivasis then were as wary as they are today of accounts–documents–deeds–laws. Hence the adivasis of Jhujhar don't even know when they once owned their own land. When they could bring the harvest of their own labour home.

The village is bound in the shackles of *betbegari* to Uttamchand. For the past few generations. To repay the unrecorded debts of their forefathers, year after year, at harvesting time, they trudge twelve miles to Uttamchand's village, Tahar, and, in return for a meal and a handful of crop, offer *begar* or wageless labour. The crop-share that they get is added to the debit side of the accounts ledger. They didn't even know that *betbegari* was illegal. They found out courtesy the Inspector of the Adivasi Office. But they did not stop giving *betbegari*. Because they knew that it was impossible for them to take Uttamchand, who extracted *betbegari*, to court. Is it feasible to go all the way to Daltonganj just for this? What about a lawyer? Someone to advise and counsel them? The Adivasi Welfare Office is beyond their reach, too. The office is in town. They are in the

village. This is not a large village situated on the rail or
bus routes. This village consists of seventy-six people
belonging to seventeen families. Until the third election
after independence, the government did not even know
of their existence. They have been voting since the
fourth election. Election times are good times.
Uttamchand says—Why go all that way to cast your vote?
Take a rupee each, my fathers and mothers. I'll vote on
your behalf.

From the fourth election onwards, this was the
prevailing arrangement. But everything changed in '77.
The teacher at the closest primary school, Balkishan
Singh, began to frequent Jhujhar village. He wheedled
and coaxed them into sending three boys from the
village to school. He explained that the sixth election
was an important affair. They must cast their own votes.
Money per head? Balkishan's efforts had brought them
projects worth much more. A panchayati well in Jhujhar
village. Huge well, lots of water. Till now, water had
been carried from the river, and in summer one almost
died fetching water.

Uttamchand first took offence over this matter of
the vote.

A new ministry after the vote. The old offices and
old officers reborn in new roles. The only road to
Jhujhar village is a footpath. The youth-team came down
that path, and noted down the particulars of those
families who were loing *betbegari* to repay debts. Purti
Munda was the mo t *vocal* personality of the village. He
was the only person in the entire village who had been
to Ranchi and Daltonganj, and vorked as a coolie in
Dhanbad. Since his financial condition remained
unchanged, he spat upon the outside world and

returned to Jhujhar.

He said—What's the use of asking us? Everything's written in Uttamchand's book. You're the ones who write things down.

—Do you know that *betbegari* is illegal?

—What's the good of our knowing that? If we don't do it, the *mahajan* won't give us loans.

—The *mahajan* will be dealt with now.

—See what you can do.

—Come with us.

—Let's go.

In front of Purti Munda, the youths tell Uttamchand, From this year onwards, no adivasi in this area will give wageless labour. If anyone is forced, we'll make sure he gets legal redress.

—As you say, Uttamchand answers, and is forced to abide by this order in practice, too. He couldn't even prevent the Jhujhar dwellers from farming his land. The youth-team told him—These people have been cultivating the land for more than twelve years. They have a right to half the crop.

—Half is mine.

—When the crop is harvested, our *samiti* will divide it in your presence.

—As you say.

Purti Munda said, all at once—Give us two bucks. Let's drink some toddy before we go home. What kind of a day is this, anyway? Whose was the first face we saw on waking up?

The youngsters said—No. Give up drinking. This addiction is what destroys the adivasi.

On the way home Purti Munda spent the eight annas he had tucked into his waistcloth on toddy, and stroking the earthen *bhand* said—Destroys! What do the babus know? How else would we forget the burning hunger in our bellies?

Uttamchand accepted the defeat, but vowed to avenge himself. He said—I'll kill them by salt.

Only he can make such an arrogant proclamation. Because the people of Jhujhar buy their necessities from the markets at Palani or Muru. And all the grocery shops in these markets belong to Uttamchand.

Uttamchand said—Let them find out what *ghato* tastes like without salt. What *nimak haraami*—after being fed and clothed by me for so long, how dare they bite the hand that feeds them!

At first, Purti and the others didn't give much importance to the unavailability of salt in the market. When it hit them, they rushed to Daltonganj. To the youth-team office. One of the boys sat in the office, listening to the transistor. He heard them out and said—This isn't within our jurisdiction. If the shopowner won't sell to you, what can we do? We're having to rush off in all directions now. With much bigger problems.

There was not, never has been, any give and take between the ideas of the babus and those of Purti. Purti just could not explain that their lives were impossible without salt. That their *ghato* was flavoured with salt alone.

Fearing the worst, they pooled their bus fare and bought ten kilos of salt. And walked eighteen miles to the village. Then they distributed the salt to all the households in the village and said, 'Use it sparingly.'

But ten kilos of salt are neither infinite nor eternal. This time Purti caught hold of the *thikadar* of the Forest

Department—Give us work. Pay us in salt, not cash.

—Salt?

Despite many steep price hikes, salt is still the cheapest commodity in India, so this proposal to work for salt makes the contractor blink. He feels the need to find out more about these people. Since they farm Uttamchand's land, he goes to Uttamchand. What he learns convinces him that they are nothing but trouble-makers. Get the militant urban youth on their side and then negotiate revolutionary contracts with the merchant they've dealt with for years! If he gives them work, he'll certainly be in hot water. Hence, the contractor shoos away Purti and the rest; and, heads hanging, the black-skinned people walk away across the white sands.

After this, in the harvesting season, they try to get salt in exchange for crops. Result—the crop is bartered away for a few handfuls of salt. Now, everyone accuses Purti—They told you to go to the *mahajan* and you trotted off obediently? How will you arrange salt for us? Trying to prove your manhood! Become a *leader!*

—If I hadn't, would *betbegari* have ended?

—So? We'd have carried on the way we were.

—Would you have won rights to the crop?

—We'd have started fasting!

To the villagers of Jhujhar, those days of wageless labour, with no rights to the crop, seem happier by comparison. They mentally weigh the losses and gains. Dark, dirty lumps of salt prove much heavier in the balance; while an end to wageless labour, and the right to a share of the crop, come out lighter.

The village elder says—So, okay, we eat our *ghato* without salt. But why do we feel so breathless? So listless?

Everyone feels that salt is not the cause; actually, the reason for all this is that the gods are angry. The village elder sighs deeply and says—It's happening to everyone. We'll have to do *puja* at Haramdeo's shrine. Take my two pet chickens, sell them to the Forest Guard, and get some salt, Purti. Let's taste salt for a day, at least.

The Forest Guard is delighted at this amazing proposal. Says—I'll get salt from the *store*, wait.

—Even if you buy the hens cheap, you won't get them for less than eight rupees.

—Okay.

—How much salt can we get for eight rupees?

—Sixteen kilos.

—Get it, then.

Very dark, lumpy salt.

—Black salt?

—It's for the elephants and deer—what do they care about black or white?

—They eat salt? Salt?

—Yes, man. We have to give them salt-earth.

—What happens if you don't?

—They wilt.

—Where do you put it?

—There are certain spots.

Lost in thought, Purti returns to the village with the salt. Elephants and deer eat salt from *salt licks*. He is completely preoccupied with this piece of news, and does not realize that the sack of salt on his shoulder cannot possibly weigh sixteen kilos. On the day of the puja, a goat is killed and there's much feasting. Later, Purti comes and sits by the river, alone. As he drinks, he stares at the forest. Elephants graze at dawn and in the evening. They aren't seen during the day. Where do they go to eat the salt earth, and when? It's a huge forest. Purti will comb the jungle to find the salt.

The market stalls don't sell them salt these days. The youth-teams don't completely ignore this news. It's there in some corner of their minds. One of them gets hold of a Medical Representative and asks him how *omnipotent* salt is for the human body. The Medical Representative has just started practising and has had no chance yet to display all his learning. What he says makes the youth's head reel.

His explanation: Salt and water are the *inorganic* and *mineral* constituents of the body. They are indispensable for life and have an important role to play in bodily *functions*. The main salts are *chloride, carbonates, bicarbonates, sulphates* and *phosphates*. These occur as compounds along with *sodium, potassium, calcium, magnesium, chloride* and *iron, CO_2, sulphur* and *phosphorus*. In general, one can say that salt performs the following functions within all living bodies:

1. Protects and maintains the internal physiological balance.

2. Keeps the water content of the body balanced and maintains the *volume* of blood.

3. Maintains the *acid-base* balance of the body.

4. Provides vital components to the skeletal system and teeth. Salt is also essential for preserving the *proper irritability* of the *nerve cells* and muscles. It is essential for blood *coagulation*.

5. Salt is the necessary constituent of some *enzyme systems*, respiratory *pigments* and hormones.

6. Salt regulates and controls the *cell membranes* and *capillary permeability* in a living body.

So many complicated facts *further* baffle the youth
and he says—What the hell, *yaar*, did I ask you to coach
me for an exam?

—Why d'you want to know, then?

—What can go wrong if one doesn't eat salt?

—What can go wrong? If you eat *high calorie* foods
instead, you'll be able to make do with a minimum salt
intake.

—*Arrey*, there are people who have no connection
with *calories*.

—Yes, yes, Indian people don't have proper *food
habits*.

—*Arrey*, the people I'm talking about . . .

The youth realizes that all this boxing with shadows
will end in his getting a headache. The Daltonganj tea
shop is not a million *jojans* away from Jhujhar village.
But the two places are situated in two constellations in
the universe, and no matter how many songs and poems
are written about the stars in the sky, who doesn't know
that they are hotter than billions of suns, and that the
dark sky between them holds these fiery, circling stars
many billions of miles distant from one another?
Daltonganj is hot with the timber trade. Jhujhar is hot
with the deprivation endured by a few wretched adivasis
exiled from modern Bharat. To make this *terrycloth*-and-
powder-bedecked glamorous young man comprehend
the problems of Purti Munda is akin to conjuring in
thin air, an effort doomed to failure.

—Who're you talking about, then?

—They only eat *ghato*, or *maroa* or boiled *bhutta* and
vegetables or fruits or meat and fish.

—They don't eat salt? Why?

—They don't get it.

—That's a tall tale. Salt is the cheapest commodity going.

—Salt isn't being sold to them . . .

—Lies!

—What happens if those who eat only *low-calorie cereals* don't get salt?

—Who are these people? Have you seen the new *fillum?*

—No. Come on, tell me!

—*Arrey,* how can I explain to an ignoramus!

—Why else did you become a pundit?

—Salt *controls* the *fluids* in the body and in the blood. If there's no salt the blood *coagulation* will increase and the blood will become thick. The *heart* will have trouble *pumping* this thickened blood, putting a pressure on the respiratory processes. *Muscles* will develop *cramps.* Moving about will become a *strain.* The bones and teeth will definitely rot. There'll be a *general decay* of the *body.* Forget all this silly stuff! Come, let's go see the *fillum.*

The film had mighty *gunmen,* gunfights, a voluptuous *tongawalli* and Amitabh Bachchan. But after Amjad Khan was duly punished by the process of law, the youth, on returning home, his mouth stuffed with Benarasi *paan,* still couldn't sweep the problems of Jhujhar out of his mind. The next day, he went to Uttamchand's house in Tahar.

At his accusation, Uttamchand said—Earlier, the adivasis never used to lie. Now they've become real mischief-makers.

—Why?

—So I'm not selling salt to Purti and his people?

—No.

—*Arrey*, I'm not selling salt to anyone. There's no profit in salt. I haven't supplied salt since the last market. Weren't they sold salt before that? How strange! Not even a little salt? Amazing! Perhaps there's no salt left in the shops.
—You aren't selling salt? Why?
—No profit.
—Is this correct?
—Since I'm Uttamchand, a *bania* who helped the Congress in earlier times, everything I say or do has to be wrong!
—You don't understand!
—No, babusaab. Sure I helped the Congress—if I don't help the ruling party, a poor rural merchant like me can't survive. When you people told me to, I stopped *betbegari* and gave up rights to the crop. The Congress boys never told me to do all this. If they had, I would have done it. Now, how can I do what you're asking? If you tell me to sell something that makes no profit, it's coercion.
—Are they coming to borrow money?
—No, no, why should they? They're getting grain. All I got were the few crumbs that were left over.
—You know how little that land yields.
—What can I do? If the land is low-yielding, is it my fault? And you know what? Even if they want to borrow, I shan't lend.
—Why?
—Now look! When you lend money, you must realize the debt, and that's illegal, according to your *sarkar*. Look, lots of dancing isn't all there is to Ganesh *puja*. Such laws existed earlier, too. The Congressi *sarkar* kept its eyes shut. Because they understood the people's

problems. They knew that if the *mahajan* didn't lend them money, the *junglee* adivasis would die of starvation. You people don't understand that. Good! You must be doing whatever you're doing for the best. If the results are good, everything's fine. I'm not going to lend them money.

The youth concedes defeat and comes away with the good intention of arranging to start a people's shop in the Jhujhar belt at the first opportunity. The intention stays with him for a few days. Then he goes off elsewhere to settle a dispute over an illicit liquor shop, and forgets all about Jhujhar.

Despite all the youths' good intentions, Purti and his people are consigned to a saltless darkness. Purti, however, doesn't abandon his efforts. Every day he silently *combs* the jungle. The deers' *salt lick* is close to the Forest Office. Then, one day, chasing a rabbit, he comes upon the elephants' *salt lick*. It is a symbolic scene. Purti at the top of a tree, in fear of his life. Not far off, a herd of elephants, eating salt-earth. Stony salt. Scattered on the stones, mixed with a handful of earth.

—They've made a field of salt! Purti says to himself.

Then, as the sky darkens, the elephants leave. The elephants of Betla understand '*show business*'. As dusk falls, the *tourists* climb into jeeps and come to the jungle to see the animals. They are used to watching herds of elephants feasting on bamboo stalks. The elephants wend their way towards the bamboo.

After all the elephants have left, an old tusker arrives. With due warning. He shows no sign of domesticity, though elephants, as a rule, are family-minded animals. *Ekoa!* Purti says to himself, and clings to the tree in fear. Some young elephant has driven him

away and taken over as leader of the herd. Such
elephants are called *ekoa*, and the *ekoa* is highly
avoidable. There's no knowing what the *ekoa* will do.
Exiled from leadership and from the herd, his
behaviour turns *irresponsible*.
  The *ekoa* sprays the *salt lick* with urine and goes off.
Purti realizes that this is his way of doing whatever harm
he can.
  Avoiding elephant piss, he collects some salt-earth,
ties it in his waistcloth and returns home. He heats
water and drops the salt-earth into it. Tells his wife—
Tomorrow we'll check how much salt remains once the
earth settles as sediment.
  —Salt in water?
  —Yes.
  In the morning they find both salt and soil mixed
together at the bottom. Purti sighs and says—Well, it's
still salt! The bastards sell no salt at all in the market . . .
  He strains the dirty, salty water through a cloth and
eats it, tells the others, and warns everybody about the
ekoa. The village elder says—Be very careful! Remember
what happened that time?
  Everyone remembers. Every year, a herd of
elephants from Saranda Forest would come to Betla,
and then go back. Some years ago, some irresponsible
adivasi lad shot an arrow and killed an elephant calf.
The elephants, furious, encircled the dead calf, walking
around him as if taking an oath incomprehensible to
man.
  Then they began their war of revenge. The residents
of Jhujhar and Kolna villages fled. The first year, they
ransacked the two villages and left.
  The next year, they came from Saranda and killed

two coolies working in the jungle.

The third year, they overturned and smashed a bus and car parked below the Betla Forest Bungalow.

Sating their desire for vengeance on man after three years, they calm down. It was not possible to proclaim them *rogues* and kill them. Because they would always move as a herd, and the older elephants would undertake *retribution*. At present, the whole of Betla is surrounded by barbed wire. Elephants are very intelligent animals; they understand the barrier of barbed wire, and respect it.

The village elder said—Whatever else you do, don't anger the elephants. Especially not the *ekoa*. They don't forget.

Their wasted bodies had worn down the youth. They said, with ashen faces—We'll be careful. Even doing puja hasn't helped. We can't breathe easily, and bearing loads makes our limbs ache.

They were careful. They stole the salt-earth carefully. Don't climb down from the trees before making sure that all the elephants have gone—They kept Purti's instructions in mind.

Then, possibly because of the *ekoa*, the *salt lick* is *shifted*. *Salt licks* are located in two or three spots. Much later, when the equation of *ekoa* + Jhujhar adivasis + *salt lick* came in for investigation, the Forest Department had a very logical explanation.

Whether *ekoa* or herd, the responsibility for the *elephant population* rests with the Forest Department. This *ekoa* is a rascal. He pisses on the *salt lick*. He licks up the salt-earth. The Forest Department hoped that if they built *salt licks* at different places, and the *ekoa* visited one, the elephant herd could use another.

The *ekoa* was upsetting all calculations. He wandered here and there. Because he was not with the herd, his sense of time was changing, too. He'd turn up at the *salt lick* at odd hours, not just at dawn or dusk. His nature was changing. Possibly he sensed that salt-earth was being stolen. Sometimes he'd come and stand in the middle of the road, unmoving even in the face of jeep headlights. The jeep had to be turned round. Was he becoming suspicious of human beings? Was he trying to pick up human smells with the radar of his trunk?

A kind of *tension* was created in the Forest Department and slowly began to increase, centred around this elephant. Such an *ekoa* can suddenly begin to cause trouble. The problem was that, until designated and proved a *man-killer* or *rogue*, no protected elephant can be destroyed.

Everyone was secretly waiting for this tension to explode. Forest Department coolies began to say that they were scared to go to work as long as the *ekoa* was there. Spotting the *ekoa* at a distance, standing and marking their movements, they dropped their work and fled. The *ekoa* had grown suspicious. So had those who came to replenish the *salt licks*. Handfuls of salt-earth seemed to have been grabbed and snatched, nothing left, they had never seen such a thing. Who'd steal something like salt-earth? No. They didn't report it. It didn't seem important enough to report. There's so much salt in *store*.

The *elephant population* was also puzzled and disturbed. There were *salt licks*, but no salt. They, too, couldn't quite understand it. Everything seemed topsy-turvy.

The reason for all this was Purti and two other lads.

At first they were careful, very careful. From evening on, they'd remain wrapped around the topmost branches, unmoving, as if dead. Once the herd and the *ekoa* had gone, they'd steal the salt-earth. Possibly, now that they were eating salt again, their muscles were once again capable of swift and natural action, the body's *osmosis* returning to normal, the heart able to pump blood at a normal pressure with the liquid content of blood increased, and the *electrolyte* balance of the body reinstated.

Possibly. And immediately, all the slippery human cunning returns to their brains. They forget about caution. They begin to lift salt-earth before the elephants come each evening. They have no idea that the *ekoa* has seen them.

Suddenly, the *ekoa* is seen less often in the forest. It is learnt that at dusk the *ekoa* stands amid the white sands of the river and carefully watches something in the distance.

—What's he watching?

—The adivasis going off across the river.

This information is not comforting. But the *ekoa* has changed the *target* of his attentions, and this news *relaxes* the Forest Department's *tension*. However, it is announced that if anyone finds out what the elephant is up to, the Office must be informed.

After a few days, work on the *khair* trees has to be abandoned once again. Because the *khair* forests lie in the heart of the jungle, on the way to the ancient Palamau fort. It is learnt that the *ekoa* is roaming around this ancient fort.

This is the fort of the once-independent kings of Palamau. The sight of this huge, mountainous, ruined stone and brick fortress in the dense Betla forest is really terrifying. In this natural forest of towering trees it is much taller than the highest *sal*. The eye is not prepared for such a massive man-made *structure*. And because of this, the fort is a frightening sight.

The jungle coolies spot the *ekoa* close to the fort walls, prowling even more soundlessly than the tiger, avoiding dry leaves, its trunk extended as if in search of something. As soon as they see this, they flee.

Purti Munda and the others naturally had no way of knowing all this, because the moment they sensed the approach of anyone connected with the Forest Department, they'd scatter and hide in the forest. To the Forest Department people, a few grains of salt are nothing. But it was because of that salt that Purti and the others had decided not to show themselves. If the Forest Department people saw them, they'd nab them as salt-thieves. While these misunderstandings were rife, the *ekoa*, deprived of salt to lick and piss on, had embarked on a hunt for the guilty—he had understood correctly: there was some kind of link between the *salt lick* and Jhujhar. That's why he would stand and wait on the white sand, in the dark, staring towards Jhujhar. The scene is symbolic. River, sands, sky, night, Palamau fort in the background, a lonely elephant. An immortal and peaceful picture. But the only difference is that the schemes that were twisting about in the above elephant's brain did not leave much scope for releasing white doves.

A few days pass thus. Then, one night, without a single witness, the elephant tramps across sand and water and, reaching Jhujhar village, stands still by the well. Morning comes, everyone opens his door and comes out as per habit to perform the morning task, and, seeing the sun rising from behind the stationary *ekoa* beside the well, promptly closes his door and sits inside in silence, turned to stone with fear. Eyeing him through the slit in the window, Purti Munda silently prays—*Hei* aba! Let no one shoot an arrow! *Hei* aba! Let no one shoot an arrow!

No one shoots, and the elephant, seeming to have his suspicions confirmed, leaves the village, crosses the river and goes away. Only when he disappears into the jungle does everyone come out, and the village elder says—What I feared has happened. You must have been careless, he's seen you. Why else would he come?

—He hasn't seen us. If he had, wouldn't we have known, wouldn't we have seen him? Is an elephant a rabbit?

—An elephant is an ant—an elephant is a butterfly—an elephant is the breeze! Such a huge body, but when it wants, it can creep up unnoticed and squash your head with its foot, and you won't even know. You fool! You shit-eating insect! You didn't see him, he saw you. Why else would he come?

—What's done is done, now show us a way out.

—Purti! I really don't know how to punish you to my satisfaction. The adivasi who goes off to work in the coal mines or as a coolie in the town, stays away. You didn't. You were kicked out, you came back thinking yourself a know-all. And you got into a dispute with Uttamchand. A tiger. Then you led the elephant into the village.

—What's the solution?

—No one will go to fetch salt. Each of you prepare escape holes in your thatch roofs. If you catch sight of the elephant, run!

Purti says—Shall we cut down thorny bushes and build a fence? They do it in the jungle. Elephants are scared of them.

—Yes, yes, in a village on stony ground! Where'll you build the fence? Which side will you protect?

—Then?

—Don't steal salt. Maybe that'll make him forget.

Purti and the rest obeyed the village elder. They didn't go to steal salt any more. Strangely, the elephant didn't come back, either. One day Purti said to the Forest Beat Officer—That *ekoa* had come to the village the other day. We were very scared.

—So were we. I don't see the fellow any more. Maybe he's gone.

Everyone felt that he really had gone. As if the dusky animal had melted into the green forest. An animal census is taken by counting pug-marks on the banks of water bodies. Without bothering to check the water bodies or ponds, the Forest Department declared that the *ekoa* had disappeared.

From the bend in the river, where the bamboos swept the ground, the *ekoa* watched everything and tried to comprehend the situation. No hands touch the *salt lick* any more, no longer does the impure scent of man cling to the air. Is this a new strategy of attack? It was as if he was realizing that man is *basically* an *irrational* being. It is an *irrational* act to anger the *ekoa* and take salt-earth. It's *rational* not to do this. But man can't do logical things for a sustained period. It was as if the *ekoa* knew that Purti and the others wouldn't be able to, either.

Purti and the rest ultimately did act *irrationally*. And the most amazing thing is that a week before they did,

Uttamchand had decided '*Enough is enough*' and had begun to sell salt wholesale in the market. No one knows whether Purti and the others knew of this. Perhaps they didn't know. Perhaps they'd heard, but didn't believe that Uttamchand would sell them salt. Perhaps they were enticed by the idea of stealing salt-earth from under the *ekoa's* nose or by fooling him. Perhaps they thought this an act of great courage, one that would establish their virility and their status as achievers. Perhaps. Or maybe they felt like *outwitting* the Forest Department. No one knows what was in the minds of Purti and the rest. But after prolonged interrogation it is learnt that before dawn broke, Purti and two other youths left with sacks. They left saying— Watch it, watch it, wife, don't raise your voice. We'll go and come carefully. The elephants leave at sunrise, we'll go then.

They go, and the *ekoa* makes its move. The elephant is the largest animal that walks the earth. But when a rogue elephant starts a battle of wits with man, then, if he so desires, he can make less noise than an ant. He carefully side-steps each dried leaf. With unbelievable caution. So, when Purti turned around, it seemed to him as if the ancient Palamau fort itself was coming towards them. From very close, an elephant looks even larger than it really is.

The elephant attacked in silence, but the three men shrieked and shrieked. At their screams, the distant elephant herds grow restless, the deer start and plunge off. The human shrieks are swiftly felled into total silence. Then, the elephant rends the sky, trumpeting in almost human glee, and stamps off, trampling the forest underfoot.

What Purti and the others had to say about why this
happened will never be known. Smashed, trampled
human bodies cannot give evidence or bear witness.

—They died trying to steal salt-earth? Salt-earth?

Everyone thinks the same thing, and the behaviour
of Purti and the rest seems completely
incomprehensible. Finally, the *daroga* says—They must
have been drunk.

No one complicates matters by wondering aloud
whether it is usual for adivasis to be drunk early in the
morning. This matter of stealing salt-earth is so
incomprehensible! A thing as cheap as salt! Why would
Purti and the others do such an *irrational* thing unless
they were drunk?

—They died trying to steal the elephant's salt-earth!
These few words uttered by the *daroga* becomes their
epitaph, and it is proved finally that the inhabitants of
Jhujhar can by no means be trusted. The herbivorous
animal needs salt, and now man steals even that! This
unnatural act reminds them once more of how difficult
it is to protect wild animals from the greed of humans.

Without his knowing it, the *ekoa* is *declared* a '*rogue*',
and because his death will not anger the herd, as he is a
loner, a *commissioned* hunter shoots him dead. The event
makes a short item in the newspapers, and even the
Jhujhar villagers turn up to see the dead *ekoa*. Looking
at the elephant, the village elder is dimly aware of the
fact that none of this is quite right. The apparent truth
is that the elephant died because it killed Purti and the
others. But the underlying truth seems to be something
else. All this because of mere salt! They couldn't get salt.
If they could buy salt, three men and one elephant
would still be alive. Someone else was responsible,

someone else. The person who would not sell the salt? Or some other law? Some other system? The law and the system under whose aegis Uttamchand's refusal to sell salt is not counted as a crime? Because his thought process is hazy and because his stock of words is limited, he cannot explain anything to anyone.

—This is not right. He tosses just these few words in the direction of the babus, and then leaves with the other villagers, and, walking single file across the white sands, returns to Jhujhar, shaking his head. He knows that the babus will never understand how salt can become something to risk one's life for, that this business will always remain unreal to them. And because he knows this, he doesn't look back, not once. Across the breast of the sands, their figures gradually grow smaller. They walk fast. They will feel at ease only when they return to their own life, a life in which there is no disbelief, no easy explanation for the deaths of Purti and the others, no attempt to deny the reality of their *existence* with simple explanations. That life.

glossary

Amitabh Bachchan: film star, super hero
betbegari: wageless labour
bonga: lesser tribal spirits, malign and threatening
Dhumavati: an angry and aggressive manifestation of the
    goddess Durga.
dibri: small oil lamp
gaona: ceremony at puberty, after which a child bride is sent
    from her parental home to her husband's house.
'*Gokulwale sawarya*': line from a popular Hindi film song
'*Mehbooba, Mehbooba*': line from a popular Hindi film song
aamrood: guava
alpana: ceremonial and decorative patterns drawn on the
    floor
Ashad: Bengali month of the rains
awtar: incarnation
Baba Vishwanath: Deity in the Shiva temple of Varanasi
baiji: singer courtesan
bakshish: tip, reward
bathua leaves: bitter edible leaves
BDO: Block Development Officer
begari: form of bonded labour for little or no pay

bel: a tree, the leaves of which are used in Hindu sacred rites

bhaiya; brother

bhand: clay pot

Bharat: India

Bharat *sarkar:* Indian government

Bharatvarsha: country of Bharat

Bharatvasi: inhabitant of India

beedi: cheap, indigenous smoke

bigha: traditional unit of land measurement, one-third of an acre

chachera bhai: father's younger brother's son

chakmaki: fire made from rubbing flintstones together

chana: chickpea

chauki: divan

chowkidar: guard

chutti leaf: loosely rolled, long country *beedi*

Commnis : Communist

daroga: Police Officer in Charge

daru-uru: booze

Decade of Liberation: the '70s, during the Naxalite movement

deota: lit. god, common term of respect

devata: same as above

Devipaksha: fortnight of the gods; the period in Autumn between Durga and Kali puja

dharma: belief, faith, religion

dhokra: indigenous bronze casting technique

dhoti: undergarment for men, wrapped around and between the legs

diku: foreigner or outsider according to the tribals

Dol: festival of Holi

Dushera: Last, climactic day of the ten-day festival season

ghato: gruel, mash, poor man's food

ghee: clarified butter

ghunshi: a goodluck charm usually worn around the waist on a length of black or red thread

gond: tribal

gulabjamun: sweetmeat

gwala: milkman caste
Haan, hujoor: yes, master
haat: weekly village market
Haathi Mere Saathi: Popular Hindi film
haija: cholera
hakim: doctor of indigenous medicine
Haramdeo: Chief tribal god
harijan: untouchable
haveli: mansion
hujoor: term of respect
Indiraji: Indira Gandhi, Prime Minister of India
ishwar: god
Janmashtami: Festival celebrating the birth of the god
    Krishna
janta sarkar: people's government
jilipi: deep fried sweetmeat
jojan: outdated unit of measurement for distance
jotedar: Tenant with secure, heritable, tenancy rights over
    substantial amounts of land. Mainly employs
    sharecroppers, who traditionally bear all the costs of
    cultivation and pay a half-share to the jotedar. Major
    institution of feudalism in the Palamau area.
junglee: wild, uncultured
kayathi: local variant of Hindi, used for legal documents
Kaamdhenu: mythical cow that grants all wishes
Khandav Forest: forest in the Mahabharata
khhichri: gruel of rice and lentils
khol: outer layer of grain, etc
kisaan: peasant
kissa: gossip, juicy story
Kshetrapal devta: folk gods who guard the fields
kunjra: wholesale purchasers of fruits, etc
Kurukshetra: epic battle in the Mahabharata; thus, any family
    feud, big fight, etc.
Lakshmi-Janardan: The goddess Lakshmi and her spouse
    Vishnu
lala: merchant, trader, moneylender
lichi: fruit

maal: stuff
machaan: platform
mahajan: moneylender
mahapundit: learned man
mahout: person who tends elephants
mahutiya: occupation of tending elephants
mandir : temple
maroa–sattu: maize powder ground to paste
maun: maund, traditional unit of weight
mela: fair
mere laal: my dear
mere yaar: my friend
mohant: head priest
moua: spirit brewed from the mohua tree.
nahin: no
nasbandi : vasectomy
Naxal and JP movement: Naxalite movement; J. Prakash
   Narayan's social protest movement
nimak haraami: lit. betraying the salt, or biting the hand that
   feeds you
paan: betel leaf
pahaan: tribal priest
panchayat-*pradhan:* head of the village panchayat
paniphal: water chestnut
panjika: almanac giving details of auspicious matters
paratha: layered, fried bread, a delicacy
pedha: sweetmeat
prasad : consecrated offerings
*puj*a: worship
putush: lantana bushes
Rathayatra: Chariot festival
rickshaw-wallah: rickshaw puller
rossogolla: sweetmeat
Saibaba, Balak Brahmachari, Ma Anandamoyee,
   Mohanananda: god men and women
Santoshi Ma: a goddess
sannyasini: female ascetic
sarifa: custard apple

sarkar: government; term of respect
sarkari-bandobast: government organization/arrangements
sattu: cheap food; grain flour
Sengel-da: lit. fire-rain. According to the tribal creativity
    myth, God sent a rain of fire to destroy creation before re-
    peopling earth.
sevak-sevika: those who serve
sipahi: foot soldier
Socalis: Socialist
thana: police station
thana daroga: officer in charge at police station
thikadar: contractor
tilak : auspicious anointment
toli: settlement, ghetto
tongawali: woman driver of a horse- or ox-drawn cart
Trimurti Bhavan: Nehru residence in New Delhi
ulgulan: Birsa Munda's movement
vakil: lawyer
yagna: religious rite

Spivak - In Other Worlds

Not taught in U.S. Academy